The Good, The Bad, And The Scandalous

The Heart of a Hero Series

Cora Lee

The Solemnization of Matrimony from *The Book of Common Prayer*, 1662

ISBN 9781944477042

Published in the United States by More Than Words Press

Cover by Erin Dameron-Hill at EDH Professionals.

Editing by Jude Simms.

To my grandfathers, Sydney and James, who passed down their left-brainedness to me.

WHAT IF YOUR favorite superheroes had Regency-era doppelgangers? And what if a group of them were recruited by the Duke of Wellington to gather intelligence for him during the Napoleonic Wars while they protected their own parts of the realm?

You'd get The Heart of a Hero series.

Chapter One

London, August 1812

SARAH SHIPTON HALTED on the stairs to the offices above the bookshop her parents—correction, her *mother*—owned. She could hear the sound of quiet weeping, yet the sun had barely cleared the horizon and no one was due in for at least another hour. She tiptoed up the rest of the stairs with her skirts clutched in one hand, pausing at the top to listen again, forgetting all about the odd man who had followed her for half of her walk to the shop.

"Oh, Thomas..."

The voice belonged to her mother and a flash of understanding lit Sarah's mind. Her father had died six months ago and though Mrs. Shipton had calmly taken the reins of their business, she was still occasionally overcome by grief.

Sarah snuck down to the bottom of the stairs then once again made her way to the landing, this time with heavy footsteps. By the time she entered the clerk's room where her mother was sitting, Mrs. Shipton had wiped her tears away and blown her nose. Her eyes were still red and swollen, but Sarah pretended not to notice.

"Mother! I didn't expect to see you here so early this morning." Sarah kept her tone light and hoped she sounded surprised.

Mrs. Shipton smiled at her daughter. "I didn't expect to see you here, either. I thought for sure you'd be sleeping in today after arriving home so late last night."

Sarah's mouth curved into a smile of her own. She'd spent the past month visiting her aunt and cousins in Dover, enjoying the summer sun...and the company of the local squire's steward.

"You know I'm no good at lying about all day. I thought I would go over the accounts this morning, then help Mr. Higgins with the new inventory."

"Oh." Mrs. Shipton's face crumpled and Sarah watched her mother struggle for several painful moments to bring her emotions under control. "I don't know how to say this, but...there is no new inventory."

"Nothing new today?" That was odd. There was always something coming into the shop—second printings of popular books, the newest Minerva Press novel, special orders for customers who wanted something particular.

"Nothing new at all."

"Why not?"

Mrs. Shipton reached out and took her daughter's hand as tears dripped down her cheeks again. "The bookshop has been losing money for months. The only thing that kept us in business was the savings your father had put aside and your dowry. Both are gone now."

Her dowry and the bookshop? That couldn't be right. It would mean Mrs. Shipton had lost Sarah's whole future in addition to the bookshop. "Are you saying that we have nothing?"

Mrs. Shipton nodded. "We have money enough to live on until the end of this month. After that..." She bowed her head against Sarah's arm and cried.

"Mother, what are you talking about?" Sarah asked the question as gently as she was able, but her mother wasn't making any sense. Sarah had personally kept the ledgers for the shop since her father died six months before, and had a hand in them for years prior. Everything had appeared to be in order.

"I'm so sorry," came the muffled reply. "I should have told you sooner. Now it's too late and we'll end up in the workhouse."

No, no, *no*. Sarah would do anything to keep that from happening...if it was even true. "The shop was making money when I left for Dover. What's happened since then?"

Sarah felt her mother take a deep breath and lift her face. "I made up a false ledger for you to work in when your father died and the shop began to lose money. And I hid some of the bills so you wouldn't worry about our finances."

False ledger? Hidden bills? "Then we really do have nothing."

And Sarah's whole future took on a shade of bleakness she'd only ever read about.

Mrs. Shipton nodded again, releasing her grip on Sarah to cover her face with both hands. Sarah rubbed her mother's back as her mind spun through possible solutions—she would deal with her mother's duplicity later. Her father was kin to a timber merchant in Birmingham, but there had been some sort of falling out and she was sure they'd find no help there. Her aunt in Dover was widowed and lived on a small annuity that only just met her needs, while Sarah's cousins worked to provide everything beyond the basics. They might be able to house Sarah's mother for a short time if Mrs. Shipton sold or let her house, but Sarah would have to find work quickly to keep from depleting her aunt's meager resources.

"Diana's ball." She hadn't meant to say the words aloud, but they popped into her head and out of her mouth with a tinge of despair. Diana Talbot had been Sarah's closest friend for the past nine years, and she was celebrating her recent betrothal with a ball given by her godfather, the Marquess of Preston. Sarah had been looking forward to the event for the past month, but how could she go now?

"Diana's ball," Mrs. Shipton repeated, lowering her hands into her lap. "It's tonight, isn't it?"

"It is."

"And your dress has already been paid for."

Where was her mother going with this? "It has."

"Then we have one hope left." Mrs. Shipton's eyes widened. "You can play Cendrillon and enchant a prince, a husband with wealth to save us."

That explained it—she'd been reading Perrault again. The story of Cendrillon and the handsome prince was one Mrs. Shipton had read to her daughter countless times in her own English translation when Sarah was younger, then in the original French as she grew older. It was naught but a fairy story, yet the happy marriage for the little cinder girl had captured Mrs. Shipton's heart.

"I doubt I'll enchant anyone in an evening, Mother."

"You are worried about your age and your dowry, but you forget that you are the great-granddaughter of an earl. You are every bit as well bred as Miss Talbot and her friends, and your education is far better than theirs."

At seven-and-twenty Sarah was no longer in the first blush of youth, and her lineage was less impressive among the *ton* than it was among her fellow shopkeepers. Combine those facts with her sudden lack of a dowry and she'd be lucky to find any husband at all, let alone a wealthy one. But her mother was right about her education, and her ability to run the bookshop should transfer well to running a home of any size. She would simply have to find a gentleman who valued such things.

Sarah gave herself a mental shake. How easy it was to become wrapped up in her mother's daydream. The far more practical plan would be to obtain a position as a clerk—if anyone would hire a female clerk—or a shop girl, or even a governess.

But aloud she said, "Yes, of course." The idea of Sarah meeting and marrying Society's equivalent of a handsome prince seemed to calm her mother, despite its improbability.

"Good." Mrs. Shipton sighed and wiped her eyes, her smile returning. "Then it's settled."

"Might I have a look at the ledger, Mother?" Sarah asked. "The real one, please. I'd like to see for myself what happened."

Her mother disappeared into the small back room and reemerged a few moments later with an account book the same size and color as the one Sarah had been poring over for the last several months. "Her you are, my dear. Though why you want to wade through all those numbers now is beyond me."

Though Mrs. Shipton had been a competent bookkeeper when her husband was alive, it was Sarah's father who had most often tended to the bookshop's finances. It was therefore possible that her mother was mistaken about how bad the situation was, and perhaps there was still a way to rescue the shop and keep their livelihood.

Sarah didn't say any of that aloud, though. She simply thanked her mother and collected the account books, taking them downstairs to study at the counter when there were no customers needing help.

But three hours later Sarah was no closer to saving the shop than she'd been when she arrived. The bell over the door *ting*ed and Diana entered, grinning and holding her arms out to her friend.

Sarah emerged from behind the counter to embrace her. "You're up early."

The contrast in their daily schedules was a running joke between them, and Diana chuckled. "I've been haunting the bookshop waiting for your return. I need your help making some last minute decisions for the ball."

"I'm so glad you're here," Sarah replied, giving her friend a tight squeeze before releasing her. "I could use your help as well."

"You first," Diana said, allowing Sarah to lead her to the counter. "Is it that steward you wrote me about?"

Sarah allowed herself a brief moment to picture him in her mind, walking her to her aunt's home. Then she pushed the thought away. "No, it isn't him. It's the shop." She glanced around to make sure the vicinity was empty of listening ears and lowered her voice. "I know it's vulgar to speak about money, but mother and I are about to lose our livelihood."

She told Diana about the shop's finances, gripping her friend's hand when she explained her mother's deceit with the false ledger. "I just can't believe she kept this from me—for six months! Even if I couldn't have helped the situation at all, I had a right to know what was going on. This affects my life just as much as it does hers."

"And now it's too late to save the bookshop."

It wasn't a question, but Sarah nodded anyway. "I think so. We can't afford to keep it open more than a few weeks, and that hurts almost as much as my mother's duplicity. My father opened this place just before I was born. I spent more of my childhood here than I did at our house."

"You poor dear. And here I was overwrought because the florist didn't have enough red roses for the ball."

Sarah managed a smile at that. "But red roses are your favorite."

"Yes, but I don't have to worry about living on the street." Diana reached out with her free hand and took Sarah's, squeezing them both. "You know I will help you any way I can."

But they both knew she could not offer enough money to alleviate the problem, having no coin to her name but the pin money her father allowed her. Her father or fiancé might help, but neither knew the Shiptons well enough to extend such an offer. It was not the done thing to speak of such matters with mere acquaintances.

"I do know, and I am grateful for it. I will certainly need your support in the coming days."

"That I will always give you."

"Good. I'm going to be in particular need of it after your ball. My mother has it in her head that I'll meet a wealthy gentleman who will marry me and solve all of our problems."

Diana giggled. "Wouldn't that be marvelous?"

Sarah sighed softly. "It would certainly take some of the weight from my mind. But I always wanted a marriage like my parents had—an affectionate partnership. I don't know if that could be achieved with a man I only just met, especially if he has to rescue me financially."

"It's not out of the realm of possibilities, though." The bell over the door sounded again as a customer entered, and Diana released Sarah's hands. "I shall return home and search through the guest list for some likely candidates."

"Diana..."

"If you find someone, your worries are over. And if you don't, well, there's no harm in trying."

Sarah bid her farewell and helped the new customer with a special order he'd placed, mulling over Diana's words. Perhaps it wouldn't be so bad to have a look at the gentlemen attending the ball. If her expectations were nonexistent to begin with, she couldn't be disappointed.

Andrew Elliott, Earl of Hartland ran a hand over his face as he entered Shipton's Books. He knew he looked presentable because his valet had refused to let him leave the house that morning without a bath and a change of clothes. Hart felt like something left behind on the boot scraper, though. The bright sunlight aggravated the pounding in his head, his empty stomach hovered somewhere between nausea and hunger, and he was having a difficult time keeping his eyes open. He'd either spent the past three days in a gaming hell or his workshop, and he honestly wasn't sure which it had been.

But Shipton's had specially ordered a collection of *The Emporium of Arts & Sciences* for him all the way from Philadelphia, and he'd been looking forward to its arrival for weeks. A good book—

particularly a scientific one—would either settle his mind enough to allow him a good night's sleep or send him into another days-long spree in his workshop. If the former happened, perhaps the events of the last few days would come back to him. If it was the latter then he might end up with a new invention or blend of steel, and those could prove useful, too.

He also knew the proprietor's daughter would put aside an interesting volume or two for his perusal, and he was curious to see what she had for him today.

"Good afternoon, Lord Hartland."

"Good afternoon to you, Miss Shipton. Has my order arrived?"

"I believe I saw it in the back room when I came in this morning. Let me check."

He browsed the shelves for the few moments she was gone, then reciprocated the smile she wore upon her return. "It's here?"

"It is. And I had Mr. Higgins hold a copy of *Elements of Chemical Philosophy* for you when it came in, too. It was written by Sir Humphry Davy of the Royal Society."

Ah, she'd chosen well. Chemistry would put him right to sleep. "Davy? Isn't he the fellow who gave the paper on combining carbonic oxide and chlorine earlier this year?"

"It was his brother's paper, but yes, Sir Humphry is the one who presented it."

He picked up the book and leafed through a few pages. "Have you read it?"

"Yes."

"The paper or the book?"

Her smile widened a bare fraction of an inch. "Yes."

"What did you think?"

"I thought both brothers explained themselves in language that was easy to understand. One needs a bit of background in chemistry to appreciate the ideas being put forth, but one does not have to be an Oxford don for said ideas to make sense."

His eyes were back on the book in his hands. "Light reading, then."

"Compared to the rest of your library, yes."

Hart glanced up and caught a glint of amusement in her blue eyes. She would know about his library—she'd selected half of it for him. "Very well then, add it to my order."

He waited while she wrapped up the books for him then bid her good day, scanning the street outside the shop for his town coach. This was the last errand he needed to complete, and he was looking forward to draping himself across the coach seat for the short trip back to his estate in Hampstead.

There was no peace to be found at Elliot House, however. Hart's butler was waiting by the front door with a sealed letter on a salver.

"This came for you just after you left, my lord. It was the special messenger that delivered it."

"The special messenger" meant the letter was sent by someone in the unofficial intelligence gathering ring Hart belonged to, headed by the Earl of Wellington. The communications Hart received most often had something to do with a degenerate specimen of a man wreaking havoc in an area near one of Hart's estates. From time to time there was even the stink of treason on said specimen, and Hart was always relieved to see such men contained and dealt with appropriately. Even better when the population at large never knew they were in danger.

He handed over his hat and gloves, taking the letter from the butler and cracking the seal as he walked toward his study.

Hartland,

I haven't much time, so I'll keep this brief. A woman called Sarah Shipton has angered someone very powerful in Dover, and word has spread that this person is offering one hundred pounds to whomever kills Miss Shipton and provides proof of the deed. The proof is to be brought to a tavern called The Black Horse in Seven Dials as soon as may be, and payment will be offered anonymously. You know more people in London than anyone and it sounds as if this Miss Shipton might be there. I hope you can find her in time.

Adam St. Peters

Sarah Shipton? From the bookshop? How on earth had she managed to provoke a threat of death?

Hart scrubbed a hand through his short, dark hair and dropped onto the leather sofa in his study. He wasn't in the habit of letting information go to waste, nor of allowing ladies be killed. But what could he do here? His usual *modus operandi* was to put on one of the armor variations he'd crafted and go at the criminal head-on. But this time he didn't even know who the criminal was. And even if he did, it wouldn't matter; this criminal had authorized anyone and everyone to do his bidding. Taking just one person out of play wouldn't do any good.

The most straightforward action would be to return to the bookshop and tell Miss Shipton to leave Town. But how would he convince her to do so? He couldn't tell her about the intelligence gathering ring—only the eleven members and Wellington himself knew of its existence and they'd all been sworn to secrecy to protect each other. Perhaps he could tell her about the letter without revealing its origins? No, he doubted anyone would pick up and leave their home indefinitely based on the claims in a letter they couldn't verify.

He leaned his head back against the arm of the sofa, wishing he'd had more sleep. Or less wine. Whatever it was that was muddling his brain he now wished to perdition. Not that it would stop him the next time he went on a winning streak at cards or had a breakthrough with an invention, of course. But perhaps he wouldn't indulge again until Miss Shipton was out of harm's way.

What if he arranged for her to visit Paris? Or Milan? Or Dublin? He had friends in Dublin that could discretely see to her safety. Would she go if he presented it as her own version of the Grand Tour?

Hart must have drifted off to sleep, for the next thing he knew his valet was shaking him awake.

"I'm sorry, my lord, but you told me to make sure you looked your best tonight for Lord Preston's ball."

"What does that have to do with anything, Richards?" Hart asked, his eyes squeezed shut.

"You also told me you needed to leave by seven o'clock."

"And what time is it now?"

"A quarter past, my lord. I tried to wake you earlier, but you swung your fist at me and told me to go to the devil."

Hart turned onto his side and tried to bury his face in the leather of the sofa. "How quickly can you have my clothing ready?"

"It is ready now, my lord."

"Good man." He wasn't surprised. Richards had been with him for nearly two decades and was more than familiar with Hart's idiosyncrasies. "Just let me peel myself off the furniture and I'll be right up."

Forty-five minutes later Hart was greeting the Marquess of Preston and his goddaughter in the receiving line at Preston's home in fashionable Mayfair. He pasted on a smile for the sake of the lady and hoped he didn't look as bored as he knew he was about to feel.

Dancing turned out to be tolerable, particularly when he partnered one of his favorite merry widows and another just two sets later. Both seemed disappointed not to have secured a liaison with him, but Hart held firm. He enjoyed flirting with women, certainly, and pushing the bounds of propriety was enormously entertaining. But sometimes playing the libertine was more fun for him than actually being one, and it kept eligible ladies from thinking they might want to be the future Countess of Hartland.

"Lord Hartland?"

It was Preston's goddaughter...what was her name? Tiverton? Taggart? "Good evening, Miss Talbot. May I offer my congratulations on your engagement?"

"Thank you, my lord." She gave him a demure smile. "I'm glad that you were able to attend this evening. It means a great deal to my godfather."

"He wanted a crush for your celebration, no doubt, and the easiest way to get a large number of people in one place is to invite me." He waggled his eyebrows. "But I do wish you every happiness in your marriage."

Hart gave her a small bow and turned to go, but she caught his arm. "Might I have just one more moment of your time, my lord? There is someone I'd like to introduce to you."

He struggled to keep from rolling his eyes, but allowed her to turn him back around. If he fought the introduction he would lose more time than if he simply let it happen. "Certainly, Miss Talbot. It is your party, after all."

She kept a hold of his elbow and towed him a few steps toward a brunette in a pale green and silver gown. "Lord Hartland, this is my very good friend, Miss Shipton."

Well, here was an opportunity he couldn't pass up. Hart reached for Miss Shipton's gloved hand even though she hadn't offered it to him. "Yes, we've been acquainted with each other for many years, haven't we?"

"We have," she confirmed, taking back her hand. "Lord Hartland is a regular patron of my mother's bookshop."

"And a friend, too, I hope." Hart smiled at each lady in turn. "Are you engaged for the next set, Miss Shipton? Perhaps you would do me the honor?"

Miss Shipton's eyes darted from Hart's to Miss Talbot's then back again. "Certainly, my lord."

He took her gloved hand again and placed it on his sleeve, but instead of leading her toward the dance floor he headed for the ballroom door. Miss Shipton glanced back at her friend, but Hart leaned closer to her ear and said quietly, "I know this is unusual, but I must speak with you. Your life is in danger."

Chapter Two

Miss Shipton accompanied Hart out of the ballroom without another word, though her body was stiff beside him. He'd probably frightened her, but her silence gave him a chance to think about what to do next. Hart certainly hadn't planned to abscond with the poor woman in the middle of a ball.

He led her down a hallway, listening at a couple of doors before he found a room he was sure was empty. Pushing the door open, he pulled Miss Shipton in and shut the door as quickly as he could without slamming it.

"What on earth are you doing, Lord Hartland?" She had the sense to keep her voice down, at least —she had the most to lose if they were caught. There was only a little moonlight filtering in through the window, but he could see she had her hands on her hips.

"I'm trying to save your life, Miss Shipton."

"What are you talking about?"

He took a breath, still trying to figure out what to say to her. "You know that I am the Armored Man."

"Everyone knows that."

Of course they did. He hadn't made a grand announcement, but he hadn't exactly kept it a secret either.

"In that capacity, I come across information that is sometimes unsavory in nature."

He heard the rustle of fabric as she crossed her arms over her chest. "And?"

"And your name came up in one bit of information." Not exactly the truth, but she couldn't know about the intelligence gathering ring. "Did you recently take a trip to Dover?"

"Yes. My aunt and cousins live there."

"While you were there, you made someone very angry."

"That's not at all vague. I'm surprised you haven't wrapped up this whole mystery with that amount of information."

Hart forced himself to keep a straight face, even though she likely couldn't see his features in the low light. She'd never spoken to him that way at the bookshop, and he found he liked it. But now was not the time for flirtation. "There is a price on your head. One hundred pounds for proof of your death. Is that specific enough for you?"

"That can't be right." There was a hitch in her voice, and he hoped to God she didn't start crying.

"It is." He stepped closer to her and laid a hand on her upper arm. "The source of the information is very reliable."

"Why would someone want me dead?"

"My source didn't know, only that it was someone with a fair amount of influence."

Her head tilted downward, as if she was inspecting his dancing pumps, and she cleared her throat. "And connections to the kind of people that could fulfill such a request."

"Exactly."

"You said this person was in Dover." She lifted her chin. "How do you know I'm in danger here, in London? I'm nearly one hundred miles away from my would-be assassin."

Hart shook his head. "The person offering the bounty included a location to bring proof of your death."

"Where?" The question was practically a whisper.

"Seven Dials."

He felt a shudder run through her, and he didn't blame her for being frightened. Seven Dials was perhaps the most notorious slum in London, offering a wealth of crime and vice.

"Someone followed me to the bookshop yesterday morning. Do you think that is connected to this?"

"Was it someone you recognized?"

She shook her head. "The sun had barely risen and he stayed some distance behind me. I couldn't make out much besides his clothing, but every time I turned a corner he was there."

It could have been an ordinary footpad, or even a doltish lad who thought distressing ladies was good fun. Or it could have been someone planning to collect the reward offered for Sarah's life. "Whoever he was, he wasn't there to see to your safety."

"What can I do?"

He placed his free hand on her other arm and stroked the bare skin with his gloved thumbs, hoping the action would calm her. "Get out of Town for a while, quietly. I can ferret out the person behind all this and put an end to it, but the task will be much easier with you tucked away somewhere safe."

Miss Shipton shook her head. "I can't. My mother—"

"Take your mother with you. It will be good for her, too."

"No, you don't understand. We're having financial difficulties, we haven't the money to go anywhere at all. We haven't even the money to keep the bookshop open."

Well, there went that option. "I will send you wherever you'd like to go, for as long as you'd like to be there."

"Why would you do that?"

He gripped her arms a little tighter. "Because you aren't safe here." She was silent for several long moments—moments in which Hart couldn't see her eyes or read the expression on her face. He drew her a half-step closer to him. "Can you convince your mother to leave?"

"I-I...yes, I think so."

"Can you do it without telling her why?"

Again she was silent. But her voice was steady when she answered a few moments later. "Yes, I believe I can. Though I will probably have to tell her you are the one sending us."

"Fine." He could work with that.

"And we'll have to come up with a plausible reason for you to take such an interest in us."

"Very well. We'll think of something to tell your mother."

"And the neighbors."

He hadn't considered that. Hart neither knew nor cared what his own neighbors thought of him, but a respectable shopkeeper and her daughter would. "And the neighbors."

"I shouldn't trust you. I *don't* trust you."

That he had considered. Yes, he was the Armored Man, the one who both prevented and solved crimes Bow Street was unable or unwilling to deal with. But he was also Hartland, the bachelor of five-and-thirty with a reputation for debauching respectable ladies, who was happiest disappearing for days into the nearest high-stakes card game.

"In almost every instance, Miss Shipton, you would be painfully correct. But in this one exceptional case, you do need to trust me. I will make sure you're safe, in all definitions of the word. I promise."

She stepped closer to him and her eyes became clear in the gloom, wary but focused. "Alright."

He released his grip on her arms and took a step back. "Good. If I come into the bookshop tomorrow, can you find somewhere we will be able to speak privately?"

"I can if you come around one o'clock. Mr. Higgins will be there to mind the shop, but no one will be in the clerk's office. You'll have to come in through the door at the back, though, so no one else sees you."

Hart grinned at that, hoping she could no longer see his expression. He'd gone in and out of plenty of back doors and servants' entrances, and his grin would likely tell her why. "I will manage."

"Then I will see you tomorrow." Miss Shipton moved toward the door, but the expected rectangle of light didn't appear.

"What—"

"Shhh, I hear voices."

He crept to the door and stood behind her, trying to quiet his breathing to better listen for trouble. There were two female voices nearing the door, not with any haste but at a steady rate.

"Get behind me."

She obeyed without question, no doubt knowing the consequences of being found here alone with him. The voices were right outside the door now, and Hart managed to take a step backward just before the door swung open.

"I believe it's in here," one of the voices said as a woman entered the room. "The last time I had it, I was reading it in the chair over by the window."

"Lord Hartland?" the second voice asked. It was Lady Rebecca Barrington, the daughter of an old friend of Hart's father, and there was enough light coming in from the hallway that he was sure she could see Miss Shipton's body behind him.

But maybe she couldn't see Miss Shipton's face. "I was just, erm, having a conversation with a lady of my acquaintance."

The first woman came back into the light holding a book. It was Preston's goddaughter. "A conversation?"

"A conversation," he confirmed. "Look, my clothes aren't even rumpled."

Both ladies studied his tailcoat and breeches, and both seemed satisfied—for a moment at least.

"Wait, didn't you walk this way with Miss Shipton?" Miss Talbot asked.

"No. Well, yes. But she left me for a gentleman who promised her refreshment and I found a new companion."

"You did? Who?"

Miss Talbot came toward him, craning her neck around his shoulder to see who was hidden behind him. He tried to turn, but stepped on the hem of Miss Shipton's gown and felt her stumble against him.

"Sarah?"

Miss Shipton rescued her gown from Hart's foot and came around to his side. "Thank you for trying, my lord. Diana is a persistent one, and would have figured it out eventually anyway."

"What are you doing in a dark room alone with a man? With *this* man?"

"It isn't what you think, Diana," Miss Shipton answered in a steady voice. "We really were just having a conversation. But the subject was delicate and we needed privacy."

The light from the doorway wasn't all that bright, but even Hart could see that both women looked skeptical.

"Were you here of your own accord, Miss Shipton?" To Hart's surprise, Lady Rebecca's voice was neither condemning nor angry. Instead she sounded more curious than anything else.

"I was."

Another not-quite-truth, since he'd practically dragged her away from the ballroom and told her to be quiet about it. But it seemed to satisfy Lady Rebecca.

"You're sure nothing untoward was going on here?" Miss Talbot sounded less convinced.

"You heard Lord Hartland," Lady Rebecca said. "If he and Miss Shipton had been in the middle of something indecent, their clothing would be in disarray. Yet they both look as tidy as you and I do."

Some sense at last. Hart smoothed a hand down the front of his coat and smiled at each woman. "Then there's no reason for word of this little encounter to spread beyond this room, is there?"

"You would be doing me a great service if you kept this to yourselves," Miss Shipton added.

Miss Talbot and Lady Rebecca exchanged a look that Hart couldn't read. After a moment, though, they seemed to come to an agreement.

"Then that is what we shall—"

Miss Talbot was cut off by the presence of Lord Preston barreling into the room. "What is going on here?"

Damn and blast. Hart kept his mouth shut and let Miss Talbot and Lady Rebecca do the talking, for he knew anything he said would only anger Preston more. He felt like a coward hiding behind the ladies' skirts, but it wasn't his reputation at stake.

"We were discussing *The Mysterious Hand*, my lord, and came up to find Diana's copy of it," Lady Rebecca said.

"In a dark room?"

"We only needed to pop in and get the book," Miss Talbot chimed in. "No need for a candle when I knew right where I'd left it."

Preston persisted. "I only saw you and Rebecca come this way together. When did Hartland and Miss Shipton arrive?"

Lady Rebecca and Miss Talbot both looked from Hart to Miss Shipton, and Hart knew it was over. The truth was written plainly enough on their faces that even Preston would recognize it. Nor was there was anything they could say that would appease him, especially when he thought a lady's honor was being impugned.

"We were here when Miss Talbot and Lady Rebecca walked in."

"You were alone with a gently-bred lady in my home?" Preston's voice rose, gathering volume with each word.

"Yes."

"You thought that because she was a shopkeeper's daughter, no one would care."

Hart heard Miss Shipton make a little gasping sound at Preston's pronouncement, and felt the blood rising in his cheeks. "I did no such thing."

"You most certainly did! Diana, Rebecca, leave us at once. And take Miss Shipton with you. Hartland and I have a wedding to discuss."

Miss Talbot and Lady Rebecca scurried out of the room, chattering away at each other once they'd slipped past the door. But Miss Shipton remained beside Hart, her bosom rising and falling more rapidly now. "Lord Preston, I assure you this isn't what you think it is."

"You have been compromised, miss. Under my very roof!"

"Then allow Lord Hartland time to speak with my mother. I've been of age for several years, but my mother would appreciate being consulted."

That would buy them some time. Preston would cool off and Hart could talk to him later, explain what really happened—some of it, anyway. As long as Miss Talbot and Lady Rebecca kept this incident to themselves, all would be well.

"Especially with my father gone on to his reward," Miss Shipton continued. "Mother's been rather lost without him, and a visit from Lord

Hartland might help her feel more in control of her life again."

The mention of her deceased father and her grieving mother softened the expression on Preston's face. "Very well, then. But I expect a note from you confirming your betrothal to Hartland within the week."

"Of course, my lord," she replied. When Hart remained silent, she elbowed him in the ribs.

"As the lady says, Preston. Within the week."

Preston allowed Hart to leave the room, though the marquess insisted on escorting Miss Shipton out himself and remaining several feet behind Hart. The ballroom was practically buzzing when Hart entered it, and the volume only increased when Preston followed with Miss Shipton.

Perhaps this was not going to be as easy as he'd hoped.

"What do you think you're doing?"

Hart grinned as his best friend stormed into the library at Elliott House. "Oh good, my conscience is here."

"And not a moment too soon by the look of things." Major Francis Oliver practically stomped over to the leather sofa where Hart sat, glowering the whole way. "I thought you had a rule about associating with unmarried ladies. Yet the rumor going around Town is that you've not only associated closely with one at Preston's ball last night, but you've gone and compromised her, too."

Hart opened his mouth to respond, but Ollie kept talking.

"You're a scoundrel, Hartland. I always knew that, but this is low, even for you."

"I—"

"What is this poor girl going to do? She might only be the daughter of a Cit, but her birth is gentle enough. And I'm not exaggerating when I say you've taken away her whole future."

"Yes, I—"

"No gentleman will have anything to do with her now, and I heard her mother is closing the bookshop. Did you know that? You've behaved so badly you're driving a respectable woman and her daughter right out of London."

"They won't—"

Ollie put his hands on his hips. "You truly ought to be ashamed—"

"I'm going to marry her!" Hart finally blurted out.

Ollie's arms relaxed and his hands slid to his sides. "What?"

Hart rose from the sofa and lowered his voice. "I'm going to marry Miss Shipton.

"You are?"

"It's what you would do." Hart winked and stifled a smile when Ollie frowned back. They'd been friends since their days at Harrow, and Ollie had always been the one to rein Hart in when he was getting himself into too much trouble. Hart, of course, had often taken pleasure in reminding Ollie of that fact.

Ollie was never one to hold back, though, either. "But it isn't what *you* would do."

Hart dropped back onto the sofa. "Compromising her was an accident—I swear it was. But it turned out to be for the best. Marriage is the solution to all of her problems and a couple of mine."

"What problems?" Ollie seated himself in the chair nearest the sofa and leaned on its arm.

Hart gave Ollie a brief account of the letter from St. Peters and Miss Shipton's admission of family financial difficulties. "If we are wed her reputation will be restored, her financial troubles will become moot, and I can keep her safe until we deal with the person who put a bounty on her head."

"How will you keep her safe?"

Hart suppressed another smile. Ollie's mind was very nearly as sharp as his own and he was quite adept at working all the wrinkles out of Hart's plans.

"I'll take her to one of my country estates as soon as the ceremony is concluded and tell no one where we're going. That should lose the horde of would-be murderers."

"What about before the ceremony?"

Damn. Hart had been so caught up in preparations he'd forgotten they'd be apart for at least a few days before the actual wedding could take place. "I don't know yet, but I'll think of something. My suit of plate armor? It's mostly for show, but it's very well made."

Ollie arched an eyebrow but ignored Hart's quip. "And Mrs. Shipton?"

"She appears not to be in any danger, but I'll send her off somewhere as well, just to be safe. If she will be closing the bookshop anyway, then she won't have responsibilities here to worry about. If the shop is to remain open, I'll help her find someone to mind it while she's away."

"Where will you send her?"

"Wherever she would like. Preferably away from her daughter and somewhere no one knows her, again, just to be safe. But the lady will have her choice."

That earned Hart a nod of approval. "How will you deal with the original threat? You don't even know who sent it."

"I don't know, Ollie. My friend might be able to find more information, but I may need your help, too."

"You'll have it," was Ollie's quick response.

This time Hart let himself smile. Ollie had plenty of reasons to disavow Hart and refuse to speak to him again, but he never did. Francis Oliver was as loyal as they came.

"What about after the threat has been removed?"

Hart's smile faded and he sat up a little straighter. "What do you mean?"

Ollie leaned both his arms on the side of his chair. "I mean what happens when Miss Shipton is no longer in danger? She will still be your wife."

"You want to know if I plan to return to my old ways." Hart slid down against the back of the sofa, tracing invisible lines on the brown leather. "Yes, I fully intend to do so."

Ollie rolled his eyes. "Of course you do."

"Do you think she'll want me around any more than I will want her?"

Ollie made a point of looking Hart up and down, no doubt taking in his wrinkled shirtsleeves and the scuffs on his top boots. "Probably not."

"Then I will be doing us both a favor."

"She'll be family, Hart."

Hart sank further into the leather of the sofa. "She will."

"She'll be your *only* family. You can't sit there and tell me with a straight face that, after a decade and a half of being the last surviving Elliott, you won't think of the one other person who bears your name."

"Of course I'll think of her," he retorted, his voice sharper than he'd meant it to be. "I hadn't planned to abandon her after all, just to stay out of her business and keep her out of mine. And I might not be the only Elliott. My solicitor may yet find a cousin somewhere to inherit the earldom when I stick my spoon in the wall."

Hart's solicitor had been looking for a male-line cousin for several years now, and had widened his search—at Hart's request—to include any relative. But Ollie was considerate enough not to mention that.

"What if she refuses you?"

In addition to playing Hart's conscience, Ollie was rather adept at playing Devil's Advocate. The possibility of a refusal had never entered Hart's mind. "Why would she do that?"

"Perhaps she doesn't want to be wed to a near-stranger, or has family to go to that you don't know about, or has the ability to disappear without a trace."

"And perhaps she dresses up in handmade armor to help take criminals off the streets."

Ollie raised his eyebrows in what Hart had come to know as his will-you-be-serious expression. "The point is, you don't know her or her situation as well as you think you do. If you weren't a customer at her parents' bookshop, you wouldn't know her at all."

"You are right, of course." Hart sat forward and leaned his elbows on his knees. "I should prepare for as many possible outcomes as I can think up.

The important thing is that Miss Shipton should be safe from her would-be assassin and his minions."

"The lady would probably appreciate a note from you, as well. Sooner rather than later."

"Why?"

Ollie gave a little laugh. "Because if she doesn't have plans of her own to disappear, she'll want to know that you're working on something. It's entirely possible that she's in hiding right now because of the gossip you brought down on her. She may not even be able to work at the bookshop today, Hartland, and that's her livelihood. If you don't at least tell her you have a plan, you may be torturing the poor woman unnecessarily."

"I don't suppose you'd go to her, would you? You did promise me your help."

"I'll deliver any note you wish to write, but I will not be your proxy."

Hart drew in a deep breath and let it out slowly, running his hands through his dark hair. The less he put in writing, the better, but perhaps Ollie had a point about setting Miss Shipton's mind at ease. Plus, some things would be harmless in a letter, even if it were found by someone hostile.

"And no," Ollie continued, "you cannot ask for her hand by letter. If you intend to propose marriage, you must do so in person—*your* person."

"I shall. I will even allow Richards to turn me out properly for the occasion." Hart stood and stretched with a chuckle. "First, a note. I'll send it with a footman. I'd rather have your help with the arrangements. But what do I tell her?"

"Start with 'Dear Miss Shipton'..."

Chapter Three

"IT'S ALL OVER Town," Diana said, coming to sit beside Sarah on the powder blue settee in the Shiptons' drawing room. "You are officially a fallen woman."

Sarah dropped her head into her hands. The news wasn't unexpected, but it was still disheartening. "If only Lord Preston hadn't been so loud or so adamant about escorting me out. No one but you and Lady Rebecca would have ever known I was that room with Lord Hartland."

"Preston thought he was doing the right thing," Diana replied, placing a soothing hand on Sarah's back. "He thought he was saving you from dishonor."

So had her mother. "Lord Hartland is not going to marry me, despite Lord Preston's insistence." Sarah knew she sounded bitter, but she couldn't help it. Her lineage, her upbringing, and her father's previous fortune all marked her out as a lady, but her station was still far below Hartland's. And if his reputation with women was any indicator, he wouldn't even give her a second thought. "Nor should he have to—we truly were only talking. Not a single thing happened between us that couldn't have happened in the middle of the ballroom."

"Except it didn't."

Never had three words been more apt. If Hartland had taken her out on the terrace, or into the garden, or even into the supper room while the food was being set out, they wouldn't be in this mess.

And yet, the rumors of her nonexistent tryst with Lord Hartland were the least of her troubles. If he was to be believed, there was a person out there who wanted her dead. Dead! But she couldn't tell a single soul about it. He hadn't sworn her to secrecy, but whisking her off where no one would see or hear them implied a need for it. Nor did she want to scare her mother or Diana if Lord Hartland turned out to be wrong.

But what if he was right?

The Shiptons' manservant—who had steadfastly refused to abandon them, despite his impending loss of employment—entered the room and bowed to Sarah, holding out a folded piece of paper. "This just arrived for you, Miss Shipton."

"Who sent it?"

"It was delivered by a footman in red and gold livery, miss. He said he was to await a response."

Sarah accepted the letter with a glance at Diana. "Red livery?"

"Lord Hartland's staff wears red with gold trim," Diana supplied.

Sara studied the seal for a moment—the stylized head of a deer with an impressive set of antlers pressed into red wax—before breaking it.

"It's from Lord Hartland, isn't it? What does it say?"

Diana was practically vibrating with curiosity as Sarah scanned the words. "He asks if he may call upon me this evening."

"I knew it!"

Sarah stared at the letter for a moment more before returning her attention to the manservant. "Tell the footman my answer is yes."

He bowed once more and left, and Diana threw her arms around Sarah.

"Your troubles are over! You're going to be a countess!"

Sarah's eyes dropped to the letter in her hand and she read the words again, hoping they would seem more real this time. Lord Hartland didn't specifically say he was coming to propose marriage, but then no gentleman would. He did express his regret for complicating her situation and told her that he was "in the process of fixing it," whatever that meant.

He arrived several hours later, as the clock on the mantle was striking seven. Diana had reluctantly returned home and Mrs. Shipton remained secluded in her bedchamber, leaving Sarah to receive Lord Hartland alone in the drawing room. With her reputation already in ruins, her lack of an appropriate chaperone no longer mattered.

She positioned herself in the center of the room and dipped a curtsy when he entered. "Good evening, my lord. It's good of you to come."

He sketched a bow and took a few steps toward her. "It's good of you to receive me at such an unusual time."

"I didn't have much choice, did I?"

She hadn't meant to be so blunt, but the expression on his face relaxed. "No. But I am here to put things right, if you'll allow me to do so."

"How?"

He came a little closer, the silver buttons on his charcoal gray coat catching a bit of sunlight as he moved. "The most sensible thing to do is to marry, of course. I spent the afternoon making arrangements for the event so we can do it quickly."

Romantic it wasn't. But it was real. The Earl of Hartland was standing in her drawing room offering to wed her. "I see."

"The Archbishop was so happy to see me finally take an interest in matrimony that he issued a special license this afternoon," Lord Hartland continued, closing the remaining distance between them. "I sent instructions to the staff at one of my country estates to be ready for us, too. I can take you away from London under the guise of a honeymoon."

"Out of London presumably means out of danger."

He nodded, his chocolate brown eyes meeting her gaze. "Farther away from it, at the very least."

That was certainly better than waiting for her attackers to arrive at the bookshop. "Good. What of my mother?"

"I will make arrangements for her as well, though I'm afraid it will be safer for both of you if you are in different parts of the world."

"You want to send her away?" Sarah wasn't sure how she felt about that. Since her father died, her mother had been the one who kept Sarah's life as normal as possible. But then, she'd also deliberately hidden the state of the bookshop's finances until it was too late.

"There is a price on your head, Miss Shipton, and you are now very well known in Society. If your mother is nearby, she may be caught in an assault meant for you."

His voice was calm, but the words broke over her like a thunderstorm. She must have gone pale or looked unsteady because his hand darted to her shoulder. "Miss Shipton?"

"I'm fine." She could see the doubt in his face and managed a smile. "Truly, my lord. The idea that my mother could be in danger merely caught me by surprise."

"Then it's a good thing I'm here."

"Why *are* you here?"

His eyes widened for just a moment and he shifted his weight from one foot to the other. "I'm here to save you."

She clasped her hands together at her waist and asked the question that had been lingering in the back of her mind since Lord Preston's drawing room. "Why?"

"I'm not going to stand by and watch an innocent woman die," he returned quickly, practically yanking his hand away.

"No, you wouldn't. That's what you do, isn't it, my lord? You stop crimes and save people from those who would harm them. But why me? And why marriage? Wouldn't it be simpler for you to bundle me off somewhere, never to be heard from again?"

She knew it would, and the way he pressed his lips together told her he knew it too. Yet here he was, offering her his name, his fortune, and his protection.

"I don't know," he finally answered with a heavy sigh. "Honestly, I've been asking myself the same question, and I've been unable to come up with an answer. It just seems like the right thing to do. You shouldn't lose your chance at future happiness because someone wants to kill you and I was an idiot about it."

A cad with a conscience...and he wanted to make her his countess. "I suppose that's as good a reason as any, given the circumstances."

He leaned forward an inch and squinted slightly, studying her. "Is that a yes?"

"You haven't asked me a question, my lord."

He grinned. "I haven't, have I?" He took both her hands in his—their first skin-to-skin contact in their nearly ten-year acquaintance—and dropped to one knee. "Sarah Shipton, will you make me the happiest of men and become my wife?"

She arched an eyebrow. "The happiest of men?"

"Too much? I've never proposed marriage to a lady before, so I wasn't quite sure how to do it."

"Too much for our situation, perhaps. But I appreciate the attempt at sentiment."

He squeezed her fingers. "And you consent?"

She liked the feel of his hands in hers, strong and steady, his eyes searching her face for an answer as if she had the option to refuse him. "Yes," she smiled, squeezing back. "I consent. I can't let all your planning and generosity go to waste. And I am grateful to you for offering both."

"Excellent." He sprang to his feet and released her. "Is tomorrow satisfactory? Or would you like a day to prepare?"

Tomorrow? "Aren't there settlements to draw up? A vicar to find? A location to choose?"

"All done. That's why I was so late arriving. All you need to do is pick out a gown and tell me where your mother would like to go."

And pack. And say her good-byes. And turn over the running—and closing—of the bookshop to Mr. Higgins. And be sure this really was her best option. "Tomorrow is too soon."

"Very well. The day after will suffice." He fished inside his coat and withdrew another sealed letter. "I've written out the details here for you, including the items I asked my solicitor to include in the settlement. I'll also send a notice to *The Times*. Ollie tells me it's the proper thing to do, and it will ensure all of Polite Society knows you are safely wed. If there is anything you wish to add or change you may send to me at Elliott House and I will see that it is taken care of."

She accepted the letter and decided to open it after he'd left; she'd be better able to process the information when she was alone. "Thank you, my lord."

"Hartland will do from now on. Or Hart, if you like nicknames."

"You'll call me Sarah, then?"

"If you'd like."

So much had happened since she arrived home from Dover two days ago, she wasn't really sure what she'd like. But she nodded. Having something familiar with her in the days to come would be comforting, and her Christian name was the only thing that wasn't about to change. "I think I would."

"Then I will see you the day after tomorrow, Sarah." He bowed formally, then took her hand and kissed it before she could react. "I look forward to it."

She inhaled deeply and held the breath, letting it out as soon as he rounded the corner into the corridor. Had the Earl of Hartland become the handsome prince to Sarah's Cendrillon? Would they live happily ever after? Or would he lock her away from the world?

Either way, she'd just agreed to give over her entire life—and that of her mother—to a near stranger.

"This calls for fortification." Following in Hartland's footsteps out of the drawing room, she continued down into the kitchen in search of a meal and perhaps a cup of tea. The practicality of eating and the fact that she still could control that aspect of her life helped to push down the wave of apprehension threatening to overwhelm her.

Upon entering the kitchen, she found two footmen clad in red Hartland livery chatting amiably with the Shiptons' cook. "Your master has departed."

The shorter of the two cleared his throat as they snapped to attention. "His lordship said we were to stay with you at all times, Miss Shipton, unless he was with you himself. He said you'd been followed by some ruffian and we were to make certain you came to no harm."

"For how long?"

"Until he assigned us elsewhere."

He left her guards? She didn't know Hartland—or the threat against her—well enough to decide if he was being overprotective or appropriately cautious. But compared to everything else she'd dealt with this day, the guards were a minor complication...and an extra set of hands. "Fine. You can help me with my preparations. What are your names?"

"Benson, ma'am."

"Goren, ma'am."

She nodded to each of them and turned back toward the door. "Come along then, Benson and Goren. We have a lot to do."

Sarah sat on the bed in her chamber clutching a pillow in her hands. What she really wanted to do was crush the pillow against her chest and squeeze it until the tension left her body, but she didn't. She was wearing her best gown—the beautiful leaf green one with silver embroidery she'd had made for Diana's betrothal ball—and crushing the pillow would also crush the gown. But a lady only married the earl who compromised her once, and Sarah wanted to look her best for the occasion.

A knock sounded on the door, followed by her mother's smiling face peering around the edge. "Ready? The last of your things is being loaded now."

Hartland had sent a small army of liveried footmen to transport her belongings to Elliott house. "Nearly. Just one more moment?"

"Certainly. I'll wait for you downstairs."

The door closed and Sarah gripped the pillow tighter. Her husband-to-be still hadn't told her where they were going after the wedding ceremony or how long they might need to remain there. She was giving up the measure of independence she had with her parents and the running of the bookshop in order to turn her entire life over to a man who could do anything he wanted with her.

"Except I wouldn't have independence if I refused Hartland," she said aloud. "Nor the bookshop. That life ended when Mother made up her false ledger."

And when someone put a price on her head.

For just a moment, Sarah indulged in a bout of self-pity. Only days ago her greatest worry had been for the gentleman she'd bumped into near her aunt's home in Dover, and the valuables that might have broken in the box she'd caused him to drop. She would give anything for that to be the case now!

But self-pity wouldn't help keep her or her mother safe and alive. Standing and placing the pillow carefully back in its place, she smoothed her hands down her skirts and took a deep breath. Marrying Hartland was the only real option she had and she wasn't going to shrink from it now.

One of Hartland's brightly painted carriages carried Sarah, her mother, and Diana to Hampstead Parish Church, where her bridegroom, wearing a tailcoat nearly as dark as his eyes, was waiting with Lord Preston and two other gentlemen outside the main door.

"Who are they?" Diana asked, nodding toward the two unknowns.

"The one in the green coat looks like Major Oliver," Mrs. Shipton answered. "He's come into the shop a time or two with Lord Hartland. I don't recognize the other one."

Sarah watched Hartland break away from the group and approach the carriage as a footman in Hartland red helped her mother and Diana alight. His lordship brushed the footman away and offered his own hand to his bride.

"Right on time," he said with a smile.

She stepped cautiously from the carriage, gripping Hartland's hand a little harder than she wanted to. "You didn't imagine that I'd be late for my own wedding, did you?"

"No," he laughed. "But it was the only thing I could think of to say that might set your mind at ease."

Her lips curved into a small smile. "Thank you for making the attempt."

He drew her arm through his and escorted her toward the group of people at the church door. "I brought my solicitor to finalize the settlements, and I asked Preston to witness the document so there isn't any question as to its authenticity."

"That was good thinking."

"I'd like to take the credit, but that was Ollie's idea—Francis Oliver, my oldest friend." Hartland pointed toward the green-coated man Mrs. Shipton had indicated. "I'll introduce you before we go in. I don't have any family to contest the provisions I've made for you, but there's always the chance that someone will come forward claiming to be a long-lost cousin and make trouble."

"You've thought of everything, haven't you?"

"I hope so," he returned. He abruptly halted a few feet from their party and turned toward her, sliding his hand down her arm and clasping her gloved fingers in his. "No. I didn't tell you just how beautiful you look today. You are absolutely stunning, Sarah."

She knew he paid such compliments to a variety of women, but felt her cheeks warm nonetheless. "Thank you...again."

"It is my pleasure."

Sarah's smile widened and she allowed him to lead her toward the church door, where introductions were made and the solicitor went through each clause of the settlement with her. Once he was satisfied that she understood the document, he presented his leather satchel as a makeshift tabletop while Sarah, Hartland, and Lord Preston signed.

"All that's left now is the actual ceremony." Lord Preston slapped Hartland on the back. "I thought I'd have to drag you here kicking and screaming, Hartland, but here you are of your own accord."

"I don't show it very often, but I do have a sense of honor," Hartland replied. "And I think Miss Shipton and I will rub along together well enough."

He offered his arm to her once more and Sarah took it, wondering how long Lord Preston's concern for her would last. Preston's affection for Diana was probably the reason he'd taken such a hard line with Hartland to begin with, but she doubted he would pay much attention to her once she was safely wed.

If Hartland was right about the order for her demise, it was better—safer—if Lord Preston forgot all about her.

Sarah swept up the center aisle of the church toward the waiting vicar, her gaze level and her breathing as steady as she could make it. Hartland was only a few inches taller than she was but he carried himself like a reigning monarch, the effect amplified by the gaggle of people trailing in their wake. She tried to draw strength from the imagery, from the solid presence beside her, but it was difficult to draw strength from a man with Hartland's conflicting reputations. Who was he really—the hero or the rakehell?

Could he be both?

"Dearly beloved," the vicar began when everyone was in place.

He had a pleasant speaking voice, and Sarah made sure to pay attention, particularly when they came to the part about possible impediments. There weren't any, but she half expected Hartland to flash a big grin and say, "I object!" while running as fast as he could from the church.

He did give her a smile and made a show of wiping his hand across his forehead when there was no answer to the vicar's command to speak or forever hold one's peace. But he didn't run, and he even became almost serious when he took her hand to plight his troth.

"I Andrew John Dominic Edward Zaleski Elliott, take thee Sarah Jane Shipton to my wedded wife, to have and to hold from this day forward, for better for worse, for richer for poorer, in sickness and in health, to love and to cherish, till death us do part, according to God's holy ordinance; and thereto I plight thee my troth."

"I Sarah Jane Shipton, take thee Andrew John Dominic Edward Zaleski Elliott to my wedded husband, to have and to hold from this day forward, for better for worse, for richer for poorer, in sickness and in health, to love, cherish, and to obey, till death us do part, according to God's holy ordinance; and thereto I give thee my troth."

Hartland's grin returned the moment she said "obey." And it grew when he slid the garnet and gold ring on her finger, promising "with my body I thee worship." Sarah made a concerted effort to keep her reaction minimal, but more questions swirled in her mind. In all the excitement stirred up by her potential murder and this speedy wedding, neither she nor Hartland had thought to discuss what they expected of the actual marriage. Did he think she would give him unconditional obedience? Were they to consummate the marriage? Was he going to lock her away until she was safe again? What would happen when she *was* safe again?

"I pronounce that they be Man and Wife together, In the Name of the Father, and of the Son, and of the Holy Ghost. Amen."

Too late to change her mind now, despite the fluttering in her stomach. The vicar said one last blessing over them, then Sarah and Hartland signed the parish register—he in a bold but messy hand, she in the precise writing she'd perfected keeping ledgers for the bookshop.

Her mother was the first to congratulate her, wrapping Sarah in a fierce embrace. "I am so very happy for you, Daughter, and not just because we are now financially secure. I do believe him to be a good match for you. I've seen him with you at the bookshop over the years. He is nearly as clever as you are so you'll have lively conversations, and I think under all that immaturity lies a man who is serious about his responsibilities. He will take good care of you."

Sarah smiled at Mrs. Shipton's usual overestimation of her daughter's qualities, but it was a forced smile. She was wagering her life on her new husband's character. "I hope you're right, Mother."

Diana was next, hugging her nearly as tightly as her mother had. "Perhaps now our daily schedules will be more alike."

Sarah laughed a little, though the fluttering in her stomach was beginning to feel more like frenzied butterflies. What would her days be like with Hartland? "Perhaps they will be."

"Are you staying in Town?" Diana asked, releasing her.

Sarah shook her head. "Hartland is taking me to one of his country estates, but he won't tell me which one. He says it's a surprise."

"How wonderful! Promise you'll write to me and tell me all about it."

Would she be allowed to write, even to Diana? She was supposed to be difficult to find. "I will do my best."

"Might I be the first to kiss the bride?"

Sarah looked past Diana to see Lord Preston beaming a few steps away. Before she could answer, though, Hartland appeared at her side and answered for her.

"No you may not. That will be my honor, Preston, when Lady Hartland and I have some privacy."

Lady Hartland. Sarah stared blankly at Lord Preston for a moment, then found her manners. "But we are pleased to accept your felicitations, my lord."

Lord Preston took Sarah's hand and bowed over it, ignoring Hartland. "You have them, my lady."

She received similar offerings from Major Oliver and Hartland's solicitor before Hartland himself held out his hand to her. "We should probably be on our way."

"Yes, of course." The sooner she was out of London, the safer everyone would be.

Sarah accepted Hartland's hand and allowed him to thread her arm through his as he led her from the church. Their little wedding party followed them to the waiting carriage—a vehicle with a more subdued paint color than the one that had brought her, without the Hartland crest emblazoned on the door—and waved good-bye as they drove away.

Hartland sat beside her on the front-facing seat and turned to her with a cheerful smile. "Now about that kiss."

Chapter Four

"You actually want to kiss me?"

As Hart's countess removed her bonnet and gloves, he studied her with the same care he might look over a new horse. Not that Sarah reminded him of a horse. She wasn't the type of woman he was usually drawn to but she was rather pretty in a serious sort of way, with intelligent blue eyes and what looked to be a pleasant armful of a figure under her gown. She was a new acquisition, though, and he realized that he'd never thought much about her beyond their interactions at the bookshop.

"Yes," he finally replied. He found that he did, in fact, want to kiss her. Apart from her physical attractiveness, he was curious about the experience itself. Each woman he'd been intimate with kissed just a little differently than the others, and he wondered what it would be like with Sarah.

"I have some questions first."

"Questions about kissing?" Just how sheltered was this girl?

She shook her head impatiently. "Of course not —questions about me, about us. About what's going to happen."

"Oh." He probably should have anticipated more questions from her now that she'd had time to properly mull over her situation. "Go on, then. Ask what you need to ask."

"Where are we going?"

"My estate in Devon." They'd be far enough from Town to be safe—he hoped—and Hart could meet with his Irish contact to let her know what was happening.

"And where is my mother going?"

He almost told her it was safer if she didn't know, but that wasn't strictly true. It would probably set her mind at ease, too, to know just where her mother was being housed. "The north of England. I have a friend whose ancestral home is there, and he will keep her safe and entertained. And overland travel within our own island is less risky than going by water in the middle of a war."

She leaned back against the seat. "Good. Thank you for arranging that for her."

"It was my pleasure." He was back to telling partial truths again. He did feel good about getting a person out of harm's way, but it hadn't been exactly pleasurable to convince his friend to play nursemaid to his new mother-in-law.

"I appreciate you allowing me to tell her the truth about the threat against me, too. I know she'll worry, but I don't think I could have lied to her."

Sarah's gaze dropped to her shoes and Hart tilted her chin up, compelling her to look him in the eye. "Don't worry, Thorston will keep a close watch over her." He released her chin. "I do regret that I couldn't give you more time to say goodbye to her and Miss Talbot at the Church, though."

She glanced down at her hands for a moment and Hart half expected a tear to fall, though none did. "I hope to see them both again soon. Do you know how long we'll be in Devon?"

This he'd been waiting for. "Until it is safe for you to leave. I'm sorry I don't have a more definite answer, but there is much information to gather before we know who and what we're dealing with."

She considered that for a moment, but nodded her acceptance. "You will keep me informed."

"Of course." He noted that it wasn't a question this time. How insistent was she going to be? Would she really want to know all the grisly details of someone's plot to have her killed? "Anything else?"

"Yes." Hart heard a note of hesitation in her voice and watched her take a deep breath. "What is it that you expect of me? As your wife, I mean."

Ah, she wanted to talk about marital relations. That should be fun. "What do you think I expect?"

"I don't know, Hartland, that's why I'm asking. I've never been a wife before, let alone a countess...or a hunted woman."

"Certainly." Well, what to tell her? "I think it's best if the staff and tenants know nothing of your pursuers, though they will surely be aware that you are the new Countess of Hartland. And I will ask the lads that work outdoors and in the stables to be alert for strangers. I've done that before, so it won't arouse suspicion."

"And me?"

"You can take over the running of the house if you'd like, but I won't be offended if you'd rather not."

"That's good to know, but it's not what I meant. What happens when all this is over? When I'm safe again and have no need of your physical protection?"

His mouth pulled into a smile. "You have that much confidence in me, do you? You're sure I'll be able to solve the mystery and deal with your enemy?"

"I have to be," she replied quietly, her shoulders stiffening. "To believe otherwise is to assume I will be dead before the month is out."

"I promise to protect you, Sarah Elliott." He should have called her Sarah Hartland, since that was how Society would know her, but it was sweeter to hear his own surname. He was no longer the only Elliott. Hart reached for her hand and held it in both of his. "I swear I will keep you safe."

"Then what happens between us when I am free to live my life again? Is this to be a real marriage, or was it just a means to an end?"

Ollie had asked him a similar question—had it really only been two days ago? "We can do what many aristocrats do when they marry for property and bloodlines. We can go about our separate lives and spend time together only when necessary. You'll remember from the settlement that I've set aside an estate in Staffordshire and one in Sussex for your exclusive use, along with a generous sum for your pin money. Those are yours no matter what happens—or doesn't happen—between us."

"Yes, I remember. Is that what you want? To live your life and go about your business while I live mine somewhere else?"

"It is." Her fingers flexed in his grasp and he released her hand. "Is that satisfactory to you?"

"Yes, I believe it is."

He studied her face, looking for any hint of feeling or reaction to their new agreement, but he found the same businesslike expression she'd worn when waiting on him in her parents' bookshop. "I would prefer that you not take a lover until you've presented me with an heir, though. If anyone is going to inherit Hartland, he should be an Elliott by blood, not just by name."

She sucked in a little breath and he smothered a laugh. There was the shock he'd been expecting.

"You require an heir?"

"Well, I don't *require* one," he told her, leaning back against the seat cushion and stretching his arm across the top. "My titles and the entailed property will return to the crown if I die without a son, as I have no other family. It would be better for the tenants if there was someone with a vested interested looking after the property, but it wouldn't break my heart to be the last Earl of Hartland."

She arched one eyebrow at him with a suspicious air, and he felt compelled to explain himself further. "Hartland is the legacy of my ancestors, not me. My legacy lies more in the people I help."

"As the Armored Man," she added.

And as a member of Wellington's intelligence ring, but he couldn't tell her about that. "Yes."

"Do you want to be a father?"

"Do you want to be a mother?" he countered.

"I expected to become a mother after I was wed."

"But do you want to?"

She didn't answer him right away, shifting her gaze to her hands resting in her lap. "Yes, I think I do. Any children I have will bear your name, but I assume they would be in my care. They would be my legacy."

Hartland had never thought about it that way before. Did that make him his mother's legacy? "If we had children together, they could bear your name as well as mine. My fifth name was my mother's before she wed my father."

"That's where Zaleski came from," she said, glancing up at him with a small smile. "I wondered about that."

"My mother was born in Vilnius when it was part of the Polish-Lithuanian Commonwealth. My father met her there during his Grand Tour and brought her back to England as his bride."

"Not his trophy?"

"It's almost like you've met my father," Hart said, giving her a wink. "That's what everyone else thought, too, but no. He was head over ears in love with her, and she was just as in love with him."

Sarah leaned closer, and he felt her hand brush the side of his knee. "Then it was fortunate they found each other."

"Fortune or fate or complete coincidence, they were happy together." He laid his hand atop hers, wishing he'd had the forethought to remove his gloves as she had. "When I told Preston I thought you and I would rub along together well enough, I meant it. We won't have what my parents had, but there's no reason we can't be content for however long we are together."

"I hope you're right."

"And I still want to kiss you."

She laughed. "I thought you only said that to bother Lord Preston."

"Well, that too." He pulled the glove off his left hand and stroked his bare fingers over her cheek. "But I think every couple should share a kiss on their wedding day. May I kiss you, my lady?"

"Yes."

Sarah's answer was half whispered, but he didn't think she was trying to be seductive. Breathless with anticipation, perhaps? He leaned forward and captured her bottom lip before she could close her mouth. To Hart's surprise she kissed him back, a little hesitantly but with more skill than he'd expected. He broke away then kissed her again, his heart thumping harder in his chest as her arms came around his neck.

His hand dropped from her cheek to her waist and slid up her back, drawing her body closer to his. He briefly considered popping open some of the buttons that marched down the back of her gown and loosening her bodice, but Ollie had made Hart promise to be considerate of his bride, to put her needs and feelings above his own while she adjusted to her new life. Undressing her in a traveling coach before they'd even left the confines of London was probably not going to do that.

He settled for one more kiss before breaking away to catch his breath. She held on to him, not quite panting but definitely not composed, her eyes fluttering slowly open.

"My felicitations on this happy occasion, Lady Hartland," he said softly.

She moved away from him—a mere handful of inches, but the distance sparked a vague uneasiness in the back of Hart's mind—and returned her hands to her lap. Then her red lips curved into a smile. "And mine to you, my lord."

"You can't be in here."

The woman looked up from the notebook she'd been studying—the notebook full of her late fiancé's careful handwriting—to see Robert MacDonald enter the room. If all had gone to plan, Robert would have become her brother-in-law in just a few weeks.

"This was my laboratory, too, Robert."

"You may have spent time here with David, but it was never yours."

Of course he would think that. Robert refused to believe that she had been his brother's partner despite the fact that she'd worked side-by-side with David for two full years before their betrothal.

They'd planned to save the world and end the wars raging across two continents. Together.

"I need David's notes," she said instead. "I'm presenting our most recent findings to the Master-General of the Ordnance in a week's time."

"*His* findings," Robert countered. "And if anyone is to present David's work, it should be me. He was my brother."

"Do you even know what phosgene is?" She paused for several moments, letting Robert squirm in his ignorance. The man was a genius with money, but couldn't tell an element from an elephant. "How could you hope to explain David's work with it, let alone convince Lord Mulgrave that the Army and Navy are in need of it?"

"How do you? Do you think anyone with real power will heed the ramblings of a delusional woman?"

She choked back a reply. She wasn't supposed to be the one calling on Lord Mulgrave. David was going to be their public face. He'd been a respected scientist in Edinburgh, and his sex would lend more credibility to their work. If not for Sarah Shipton he would still be with her, and she wouldn't be having this pointless argument with Robert.

Or trying to fulfill their dreams alone.

"Lord Mulgrave will heed me." She would make sure of it.

"Even if he does, you're still trespassing. This property passed to me upon David's death and I want you gone from here." Robert pulled his watch from his pocket and glanced at its face, his expression softening a little. "I know he loved you, despite your masculine pursuits. Because of that I will allow you ten more minutes with his notes before I have you escorted from this place. You will leave your key when you depart."

Ten minutes? No doubt Robert thought he was being magnanimous by not having her immediately removed, but ten minutes wouldn't be nearly enough time to compile the data from months of experimentation. Nor would he allow her to remove any of David's notebooks. She wouldn't be surprised if he had her searched on her way out.

"Thank you," she managed, casting her eyes down toward the floor. A little contrition, however false, would go a long way with Robert. Perhaps she could convince him to permit her a return visit in a day or two.

She kept her gaze down until he exited the laboratory, then looked about her. If she couldn't take David's notes with her and Robert didn't let her return, she needed another way to access the materials she required for her presentation to Lord Mulgrave.

Snatching up a leather satchel that had belonged to David, the woman stacked David's notebooks inside until no more would fit. A few glances from the windows assured her that no one was guarding the door yet. That was a stroke of good fortune. She hugged the satchel to her body and left the lab, looking for a place to hide David's notes.

She settled on an old flower bed that hadn't been planted since David had first brought her to his laboratory. Loose soil in a flower bed wouldn't look out of place if anyone noticed it, nor should anyone be rooting around there this time of year. She dug a hole with her hands and dropped the satchel inside, covering it with most of the dirt she'd excavated while scattering the rest around the bed.

When she was satisfied no one would notice her hiding place, she wiped her hands on the grass as best she could and returned to the lab to collect her bonnet and gloves. By the time she'd made herself presentable once more, a footman in MacDonald livery had arrived and politely asked her to accompany him to the nearest road. He offered his condolences on the loss of her fiancé and promised to find her a hackney to take her home.

She did her best to appear bereaved—not difficult when she missed David with every breath she took—and allowed the footman to escort her away from the lab. All she needed to do was return after dark and collect the notebooks. Robert would never know, and she would have all the information she needed for Lord Mulgrave.

Chapter Five

SARAH AWOKE HALF-SITTING, her body resting against something hard while soft cloth pressed against her cheek, smelling faintly of cloves and mint. Hartland had insisted they travel through the night, and she remembered dozing off with her head resting against the carriage window. But where had she woken up? She opened her eyes partway and blinked as her field of vision filled with white linen.

It was Hartland's shirt.

He shifted beneath her, his chest rising as he inhaled deeply then falling again as he exhaled. She felt a hand tighten on her hip and realized he'd wrapped his arm around her as she slept. Had he been conscious when he did it, or had he attempted to embrace her in his sleep?

She dismissed the thought. How they'd ended up in such an intimate pose didn't matter so much as how much longer their journey was. They'd been traveling for two days and nights, and sleeping in the carriage—even with Hartland's body to cushion her from some of the bumps—had not been pleasant. She sat up and pushed the loose hair out of her face, trying to focus her eyes on the scenery rolling by.

"We'll stop one more time to change the horses," came Hartland's voice. "Should only be a few more hours before we arrive."

Sarah glanced over at him. He was still reclining on the front-facing seat with his eyes closed, his tailcoat and waistcoat balled up on the floor at his feet. "Where are we?"

"Northwest Devon," he replied without opening his eyes. "Thirty miles or so from Hartland Abbey."

"How long have you been awake?"

"Long enough to know that you snore."

Her glance became a glare. "I do no such thing."

"How would you know?" he asked, blinking open his eyes with feigned innocence. "If you've only ever slept alone, you'd have no one to tell you."

Her eyes narrowed as she stared at him, unable to form a response that would both teach him some manners and preserve her privacy. Finally, she waved a hand in a dismissive gesture and moved to the rear-facing seat. "As if it matters to you, anyway."

The smile faded from his face. "Should it? Do you want it to matter to me?"

"No, Hartland, it's fine. We're to have an aristocratic marriage, remember? That means neither of us has to think too much about the other." She leaned her head against the back of the seat and tried to find something interesting to look at outside.

"Once you're safe, of course."

Her eyes shifted back to him. Was he trying to remind her just how much she needed him? As if she would forget that. "Yes, once I'm safe."

Sarah reached for the book she had brought with her and opened it to where she'd left off, noting that Hartland closed his eyes once again and crossed his arms over his chest. They spent the rest of the journey that way, speaking only a few words to each other when they entered the inn to refresh themselves and change clothing.

It wasn't until they pulled within sight of Hartland Abbey itself that its master spoke up again. "Home, sweet home."

Sarah dropped her book into her lap and watched the house grow larger as they approached. "It looks rather medieval."

"It is—it was built when the second Henry was king, and was a monastery until the eighth Henry gave it to one of his favorites." He flashed her what she was beginning to recognize as his I'm-very-clever smile. "Don't worry, it's been renovated extensively over the years. You'll be quite comfortable."

"I expect I shall." She straightened in her seat as they headed down the front drive, her heart sinking. What looked to be the entire staff had gathered in front of the main entrance, forming neat rows of male and female servants.

"I thought I told them not to greet us at the door," Hartland grumbled. "I knew we'd be tired from traveling, and I didn't want to subject you to something like this until you'd had a chance to get some proper rest."

"Something like what?"

"It's tradition to present each member of the household staff to the new countess when the earl marries. But it will be a long process, and I didn't want to overtax you."

Sarah took one more look at the assemblage—which appeared large enough to populate a small village—then focused on her husband. "It's a small misunderstanding and nothing more. I'll manage."

"Aren't you tired? You can't have slept very well these past two nights."

"I didn't. And yes, I am tired. But I can meet the servants before I retire. They'll be curious about me, and I am curious about them."

He shook his head, his mouth pulled into a frown. "I don't think it's a good idea, Sarah. Why don't you just let the housekeeper show you to your rooms and we'll worry about the staff later?"

"Hartland, I can do it." She said each word slowly, and made a point to enunciate them all.

His posture stiffened but he didn't argue. "Very well, then. However, we will save the tour of the house and grounds for later."

That she'd readily agree to. What she could see of the estate looked like it took up half the county, and she suspected there was more beyond view. It would take her days to see it all.

Contrary to Hartland's belief, Sarah thought she held up rather well under the scrutiny of the Abbey's staff. She even mustered enough energy to be introduced to her new lady's maid, Lucy, and to make passable small talk with the housekeeper, Mrs. Nichols, as the pair walked through the house toward the Countess's suite. But as soon as Mrs. Nichols and Lucy made their curtseys and departed, Sarah climbed onto the big bed and stretched out on her back.

For the first time in days she didn't have to worry about where her arms or feet were, or the rattling of the carriage as they bumped along. She was finally in a stationary building for more than a few minutes...and alone.

She didn't feel herself falling asleep, didn't even realize she'd been asleep until she began to wake. Taking a page from Hartland's book, she elected to keep her eyes closed for a few moments to savor her comfortable position and the light breeze blowing in through the open window. What a luxury to simply lie in her soft bed until she was ready to rise!

"Are you sure, my lord? It doesn't seem right—"

"I know how it seems, but your cooperation will be very helpful. And I'll see that you're properly compensated, of course."

The voices were coming from the direction of the dressing room at the far end of the room, and Sarah recognized the second as Hartland's. The first sounded familiar, but she couldn't wake her brain enough to place the woman speaking. And what was she to be compensated for?

"What if someone finds out?" the woman asked, the pitch of her voice rising. "What if the mistress finds out?"

"No one will find out..." The volume of his voice dropped and his words became an unintelligible murmur.

Find out what? The woman in the dressing room was most likely one of the maids. Ah, it was Lucy, Sarah's new lady's maid. She was probably unpacking Sarah's belongings and tending to her wardrobe. But what had Hartland been doing with her in his wife's private chamber?

The voices died away and Sarah counted to one hundred before pulling herself into a sitting position. The gown she'd slept in was a wrinkled mess and her hair was most certainly a fright, but she climbed off the bed and wandered toward the dressing room.

Lucy poked her head out and smiled brightly, bobbing a curtsy. "Good evening, my lady. Was your nap restful? I hope I didn't wake you with my work in here."

"No, you didn't wake me," Sarah replied, walking past the maid and into the dressing room. "I thought I heard you speaking to my husband just now, though. Where did he go?"

Lucy followed her, pointing to a second doorway at the other end of the dressing room. "Oh no, my lady. Perhaps you heard his voice carry from there—it connects to his lordship's own dressing room."

Sarah doubted very much that she'd heard Hartland so clearly through a closed door, but decided not to challenge Lucy on it right then. It was entirely possible that he'd propositioned the girl, who would feel compelled to accommodate her employer or risk losing her position. If Sarah were to press, she might make things worse.

"Perhaps I did. Or perhaps I dreamed it. I was sleeping rather deeply."

"Certainly, my lady. I understand you had a long journey."

And not just in distance. Sarah had gone from wealthy shopkeeper's daughter to woman of imminent poverty to countess in less than a week. "All the way from London."

"Are you quite refreshed? Mrs. Nichols said you mightn't want to take dinner with his lordship tonight, but instead would want a tray here. I can let Cook know—"

"Thank you, Lucy, but I believe I will dine with his lordship tonight. We are newly wed after all, and this is to be our honeymoon. I should like to spend as much time as I am able with my husband."

Sarah watched the red creep into Lucy's cheeks for a moment before the maid turned toward the clothespress. "Then let us find you an elegant gown, my lady, and we'll do your hair in a classic style. His lordship won't be able to take his eyes off you."

Hart waited in the drawing room for his bride. A little voice in his head—one that sounded remarkably like Ollie—chastised him for being too harsh with Sarah when the carriage pulled up in front of the house. His promise to Ollie to be considerate of his new countess had put a damper on his lust, and also, apparently, on his judgment. Or perhaps he was as tired as he thought her to be. He hadn't slept all that well in the carriage, either, bouncing along some of the rougher roads, trying to keep his hands from ending up somewhere inappropriate. And then he'd woken up with her head pillowed on his chest...

"Good evening, Hartland."

He pulled himself away from his musings and focused on Sarah. She stood just inside the doorway, her hands clasped together in front of her. The gown she wore was simpler than what he was accustomed to seeing during the Season, some darker shade of pink he couldn't name with only a few embellishments. It suited her, though, and Hart wished for a moment that he'd told her he did require an heir. He wouldn't have taken her to bed while trying to protect her, though. There was no telling what they would have to endure before she was safe again, and a pregnancy would only complicate matters.

"Good evening, my lady. You look lovely tonight."

She offered him a demure smile. "Thank you. You look rather handsome yourself."

Did he? He hadn't even paid attention to what Richards had laid out for him. "Thank you. Shall we go in to dinner?"

He offered her his arm and escorted her to the dining room. He'd asked that their places be laid close together rather than at the head and foot of the table so they might talk more easily. If he couldn't investigate in Town, he could at least begin gathering information from his wife.

Hart sat at the head of the large table, with Sarah seated at his right hand. Bearing in mind his earlier irritability, he allowed her to direct the conversation for the first two courses. By the time the third course was served, her expression had relaxed and her pretty blue eyes sought his gaze more and more often.

"Sarah, may I ask you some questions about your trip to Dover?"

She placed her knife and fork on her plate and folded her hands in her lap. "I suppose you'll want to know everything that happened while I was there."

He threw his napkin onto the table and leaned on one elbow. "Just the unusual things. Did you anger anyone? Offend anyone? Get in anyone's way?"

Her eyes shifted away from his. "There was a steward I met. He wasn't very happy when my aunt told him I was marrying you."

So there had been a suitor before him. Interesting. "Did he... Did you..."

"We weren't betrothed," she supplied, meeting his gaze again. "I'd hoped that we might become so, and apparently so did he."

"But the two of you were on friendly terms while you were in Dover?"

Sarah nodded. "Which means he couldn't be the one who wants me dead. Even if he was that angry with me, and I don't think he was, the timing is all wrong."

"That's right—I didn't ask for your hand until after the threat had been issued." He dropped his arm onto the table. "There has to be someone else, then."

"Just the gentleman I bumped into in town."

"Another gentleman? I'm starting to think you didn't need to marry me after all."

Sarah brushed a nonexistent strand of hair from her face. "He was dressed as a gentleman, but I'd never seen him before that day. I literally bumped into him walking down the street. He dropped the box he was carrying and I thought I heard glass break, but he insisted everything was fine."

"That was it?"

"That was it," she confirmed. "I didn't see him again after that."

Her voice was steady, her posture straight but not rigid. Odds were she wasn't hiding anything. "Couldn't have been him, then, either. The threat named you specifically, and you didn't know him. Could he have known you?"

"If he'd been to our bookshop, perhaps. But even then it's unlikely. How many shop girls' names do you know?"

"Well, let me see. I knew yours before I married you..." He let the word trail off and genuinely tried to put names to the faces he saw in shops every day. Some of the proprietors' names he could recall, of course, but not that of a single other woman who had waited on him. "Huh. You're the only one."

"Should I be flattered?"

She was smiling, and he decided it would be more fun to flirt with his wife than dwell on the gaps in his memory. "Yes." He clasped her smaller hand in his and brought it to his lips for a gallant kiss. "You are the one I chose, after all."

Her smile faltered. "I am the one who was forced upon you."

"No one forced me to do anything," he replied, lacing his fingers with hers. "Our journey to the alter may not have been conventional, but my choice was freely made."

Too late he remembered that hers wasn't, not really. His earlier harshness in the carriage nibbled on his conscience again. The deal he'd struck with

Sarah's young maid did, too. "Did you find your chamber satisfactory?"

She arched a single eyebrow at his abrupt change in topic, but nodded. "It's much more spacious than I expected. And the bed is the softest I've ever slept on. I'm sure I'll be very comfortable for however long we're here."

"Good." He idly ran his thumb over the back of her hand. "If you find you should need anything, and I do mean anything, I am at your disposal."

"Thank you."

She smiled once more, glancing down at the table. Did she think he was going to kiss her again? He wanted to, but he was afraid he'd imposed upon her enough for one day, and he had promised Ollie he'd behave. "And if you think of anything else unusual that happened while you were in Dover, tell me immediately."

"I will."

"Good," he repeated. How had this woman garnered a death threat? Yes, she had some backbone, but she otherwise seemed like so many other ladies of the *ton*. What was so special about Sarah?

"I'm sorry, my lady. This just isn't something we could use."

The woman stormed across Horse Guards Parade with the words ringing in her head. Isn't something they could use? What army couldn't use a weapon that would bring the enemy to its knees? She and David had already done the work for the Master-General of the Ordinance. They could produce the gas in quantities large enough to use on the battlefield. They could contain it within several different kinds of large projectiles, which could then bombard an opposing force. They could even contain it within smaller projectiles that an individual soldier could carry on his person, very much like grenades.

But Lord Mulgrave had refused her every suggestion. He declared phosgene impractical and ineffective and decreed that the Royal Army would have nothing to do with it.

She climbed into her waiting carriage, setting down her satchel—David's leather satchel from his lab—and banging her fists against the velvet seat. How could Lord Mulgrave not see the importance of such a weapon? Transportation of the gas wasn't easy, and it didn't kill instantly. But almost immediately it made the eyes water and disrupted the breathing of anyone unlucky enough to inhale it. That alone would disable a line of enemy soldiers long enough to take them all prisoner.

Surely with a weapon like that, Britain would dominate Napoleon's Grande Armée and end this never-ending war. How many Allied lives would be saved? How many Spanish and Portuguese people would be able to return to their homes and begin their lives again?

The satchel slid at her feet as the carriage rounded a corner and the woman picked it up. She'd brought a sampling of her phosgene grenades, hoping to demonstrate their effect on a box of rats she'd had delivered prior to her arrival. She didn't get to make her demonstration, and the grenades were volatile. It wouldn't do to have one of them break open and release a deadly gas inside the confines of her carriage.

But perhaps she could make a demonstration of a different kind.

A demonstration that was sure to get the attention of other important people within the Army's structure. One that would prove to them what an asset phosgene would be in every battle they fought.

She banged on the roof of the carriage and gave her driver a new destination when he opened the little hatch. Bond Street would do nicely.

She chose a shop at random, not even bothering to see what was being sold. She did pause long enough to notice that there were other females inside, and many of them were well-dressed. At least she wouldn't stand out. Taking a deep breath, she entered the shop with her satchel and pretended to peruse the shelves that lined the walls.

It was a bookshop.

Not Shipton's—it was closed now—but still she smiled. How satisfying it would be to make her grand demonstration in a place sacred to the woman who killed David. Not quite as satisfying as seeing Sarah herself dead on the floor, but close enough for today.

The woman discreetly removed the grenades from her satchel, concealing them among the shelves and under a table, wrapping the long fuses around the thin iron spheres as she lit them. She made sure to stay in a section of the shop that wasn't heavily trafficked. There was less of a chance she'd be caught, and people would eventually go over to see what happened. That's when the phosgene would do its work.

She saw smoke rising from one of the shelves where she'd placed a grenade. One of the fuses must have caught a book on fire. No time for the last grenade, then.

"Someone help! Something is smoking!"

She scurried to the other side of the shop as a couple of gentlemen went to investigate. A few people made for the door and she went with them, stepping out onto the street just as the first grenade exploded. She skirted the crowd that poured out of the bookshop, finding a place near the back to take in the results of her work.

It was only a few minutes more before people exited the shop in distress. One was an old woman, coughing so hard she needed assistance to remain on her feet. Two children trailed along behind her, one holding a handkerchief to his forehead, the other with bloodstains on her sleeve.

The woman sucked in a breath. Other people left the shop, some of them in worse shape than the others, but she ignored them. She followed those first three victims with her eyes, unable to look away. Of course she'd known that people would be hurt if she used her grenades in a Bond Street shop, but she hadn't thought much about it. They were just faceless strangers, their damage necessary to prove phosgene's worth and make David's dream of ending the war come true.

But these people had faces. They had voices that cried and moaned. They bled real, red blood. And she was the cause of their pain.

The woman finally turned away when the crowd began to disperse, wishing she'd followed her first instinct to run from the shop when the book caught fire—to run and not look back. Her heart ached for the victims of her work and she struggled to keep the tears from spilling down her cheeks.

If only David had been there with her. None of this would have had to happen if he'd still been alive. He would have been the one to speak with Lord Mulgrave, who surely would have seen the merits of phosgene as a weapon of war when David explained them. Then these innocent people wouldn't have been subjected to a bombing in the middle of Bond Street and she wouldn't be feeling this awful ache in her heart.

If it weren't for Sarah Shipton, none of this would have happened.

Chapter Six

THE NAP SARAH took upon arrival at Hartland Abbey turned out to be the only time she had completely to herself. In the four days since then, Hartland had taken to looking for her if she was out of his sight for more than an hour. They slept in their separate bedchambers, but his adjoined hers so he was never far away from her at night, either—assuming he was actually in his chamber at night.

As if she'd conjured him, Hartland strolled into the drawing room where Sarah sat on a sofa nestled in a sunny bay window. He acknowledged her with a nod and dropped into a chair on the far side of the room, opening the book he'd brought with him. She shook her head a little and returned to her own book, but only a few minutes later Hartland popped out of his chair and chose another.

Ordinarily, she would have said something. It would have been inconsequential, but it would have eased the slight tension hanging in the air. It was a lady's responsibility, after all, to see that every person in the room was comfortable. This time, though, she decided to conduct a little experiment and remain silent to see what Hartland would do when left to his own devices. She'd been thinking more of her mother and Diana than paying attention to her book, anyway.

What he did was fidget. For ten straight minutes he shifted positions in his chair, drummed his fingers on all the nearby hard surfaces, tapped first one foot then the other against the chair leg, and generally made himself a nuisance.

Was he regretting their marriage and his promise to protect her? Or was he simply unused to living with a person who wasn't a servant? "Will you tell me about Major Oliver? How did you two meet?"

He glanced sharply in her direction. "Why do you want to know about Ollie?"

"You said he was your closest friend, but I didn't have the chance to speak with him very much. I thought I might get to know him better through you." And perhaps listening to stories of her husband's best friend would ease the ache of missing hers.

Hartland eyed her, an expression that wasn't so much suspicion as it was an appraisal. "We went to public school together," he responded in an even voice. "He was having a difficult time with Physics and I offered to help."

"That was nice of you."

His eyes shifted away from hers for a moment and his forehead creased. "…in exchange for the biscuits and treats his mother sent him every month."

"You forced him to pay you in sweets?"

"Yes." His gaze met hers and he looked as though he was trying to suppress a grin. "It was a mutually beneficial arrangement."

"Did Major Oliver feel that way?"

"Probably not."

Sarah carefully put her book down on the sofa cushion. "How is it the two of you have managed to stay friends all these years after a beginning like that?"

"I don't know." Hartland propped one ankle on the opposite knee and—to Sarah's surprise—kept his dangling foot still. "I suppose it was because neither of us really knew children our own age when we arrived at Harrow. Ollie is the youngest of his siblings by a number of years. I, of course, have no siblings, and I suppose we bonded over that as well as our studies."

"Brothers in spirit, though not in blood."

"Something like that, yes."

"Is that why he has rooms set aside here for him? Mrs. Nichols mentioned it when she was giving me a tour of the house."

Hartland offered a smile that was almost demure. "Something like that, yes."

"Oh, come now. You can't put me off with a nothing answer. I detect a story in that little smile of yours, and I'd like very much to hear it."

His smile widened, but there was little joy in it. "Ollie was invalided home last year. He was wounded in the leg at the Battle of Albuera, and infection had set in. His parents and eldest brother were at the family plantation in Barbados, his middle brother on a ship somewhere in the Atlantic Ocean on his way to join them, so there was no one here to care for him."

"So you cared for him."

Hartland scrubbed a hand across the back of his neck and rose. "I brought him here, actually. Found the best physician to attend him, hired some women from the village to see to all his needs. It was weeks before we knew if he'd live."

This was not the brash, arrogant Hartland bragging about the good deed he'd done. There was real fear on Hartland's face, though Sarah doubted he realized it. He'd come so close to losing his friend, the man who was his brother in all but blood, and the memory was clearly still a powerful one.

"You must have been terrified," she said softly.

He wandered over to her sofa and sat at the far end of it, resting his elbows on his thighs. "I was."

"You saved his life."

"No, the physician and the women who tended him saved his life."

Sarah wanted to touch him, to put her arms around this unexpectedly vulnerable Hartland and comfort him. But she still didn't know him all that well, and she wasn't sure how he would react to such an overture. Instead she offered him what she hoped were encouraging words. "You orchestrated his survival, then. And his recovery, too, I'd bet."

Hartland reclined back against the sofa cushions, the emotion of a moment ago vanished into his usual smirk. "A lady should never wager, you know. But in this case you would have won— Ollie stayed here for nearly six months, traipsing around the grounds just as soon as the physician allowed him to do so. Have you been out to see the rest of the estate yet?"

"No." As if he didn't already know that with all his following her around.

He popped up off the sofa and extended his hand to her. "Shall we, my lady?"

She cast a longing look at the book lying beside her but decided to take Hartland up on his offer. He would undoubtedly continue to dog her every move, and if they were walking the grounds at least he wouldn't fidget. "I believe we shall, my lord," she answered, taking his hand and rising. "Where do we begin?"

After changing into her half-boots, Sarah headed out with Hartland into the valley that surrounded the Abbey and they walked side-by-side along the stream at the edge of the property. He didn't offer her his hand or arm again, and actually made a point to keep two or three feet of space between them at all times. Was he embarrassed by his earlier display of emotion?

"Have you had any further information about my situation?" It was only the two of them, and they were surrounded by nothing but countryside and animals. Surely it was safe to speak of it out here.

"No." The word was clipped and he kicked at a rock as they passed it.

"Oh." Perhaps that was why he'd been following her like a lovesick lad. He was feeling the need to do something, to spring into action, but there was no action to take just now.

Hartland continued to follow the stream in silence—with Sarah tagging along like an unwanted little sister—until they reached an old stone bridge and a pair of much newer buildings. He kept walking, but she noticed his pace slowed a little and his eyes focus on the larger of the two buildings.

"What are those for?"

He gestured to the larger of the two buildings, made from white stone with floor-to-ceiling windows spread across the front. "That's my workshop, and that—" He pointed to the less elegant building beside it, built from a dark brick that closely matched the main house. "—is the forge."

"You have a forge?"

His smile returned, this time with the sort of affection that gentlemen usually reserve for their favorite horses. "It was built sometime after the abbey became a private home. I have a smith who comes to Hartland every few weeks to make the repairs on my armor that are beyond my skill, and he works here now."

She took a few steps closer to the bridge and paused there, trying to get a better look at the old forge. "Do you ever work in there?"

"A gentleman would never dirty his hands so."

His statement was delivered in a deadpan voice and she turned her focus to Hartland's face. "You are not the average gentleman, though."

His smile widened just a fraction and he came to stand beside her, looking over the two buildings. "I might know my way around a hammer and anvil."

"I'm trying to picture you in a leather apron and heavy gloves, but it isn't quite working."

His eyebrows lifted in surprise and Sarah immediately felt ridiculous. Her mother would have been shocked by such an admission.

"Would you like to watch me work?"

"I-I would like to learn more about your work. What is your armor like?"

"I have different types for different situations," he replied, the corners of his mouth turning upward. "Some plate pieces, like the knights of old. Some made more like garments with plates on the inside. There are other pieces, other materials, scattered around my other properties so I always have something on hand in case I need it. I'll show you this workshop another time, and you can see what I have here."

They resumed their walk along the stream and, though their conversation was still sparse, Hartland's body drifted closer to Sarah's. His step was lighter, too—he was fairly bouncing as they approached the mouth of the stream.

"Do you think you can manage a climb up to the top of the cliff? There's a path, but it's a bit steep. Or are you too tired?"

She grabbed his elbow and turned him to face her, tugging him to a stop. "Queen Elizabeth may have considered herself 'weak and feeble' but I do not. I am stronger than you think I am."

"You'll tell me if you need a rest?"

"I will."

He squinted his eyes at her and pressed his lips together, but ultimately relented. "You walk on this side of me," he told her, positioning her to his left, "and don't peek over the edge. The view from the top is even more breathtaking when you don't see it coming."

A quarter of the way up Sarah was congratulating herself for wearing half-boots rather than slippers. The climb was steeper and the terrain rougher than anything she'd experienced walking the streets of London. Halfway up she stumbled but Hartland's hands were at her waist and wrist, holding her securely.

"All right?"

She tested both ankles. "All right."

He released her wrist but kept a hand at the small of her back all the way to the top of the cliff. His touch didn't provide much in the way of physical support, but it did help to spur her onward along the path.

Just as they crested the cliff, Hartland's hands came over her eyes. "Don't look yet!"

"Hartland, what are you doing?"

Her words were nearly carried away by the wind blowing off the Atlantic, and he leaned close to her ear when he answered her. "I told you, it's better if you see it all at once."

He took her own hand and placed it over her eyes, then put his hands on her shoulders and steered her into the wind. Her hair blew straight back, some of the pins coming loose before she could put her free hand to her head, and she suddenly wished she'd remembered to wear a bonnet.

"Don't look yet! Take three steps forward, I won't let you fall."

She obeyed, stepping slowly forward as he counted aloud. He hadn't gone to all the trouble of marrying her and saving her from a murderer only to throw her off a cliff. They halted together and she felt his warm breath on her ear when he leaned in again and spoke.

"Now."

She dropped her hand from her eyes and sucked in a breath. The cliff face rose out of the ocean in jagged brown edges with a thin coating of green grass across the top, and the bluest water she'd ever seen lapped at the little beach below.

"Oh, Hartland..."

"'Beautiful' doesn't quite seem strong enough, does it?"

He slid his arms around her waist and she leaned back against him, shaking her head. "I doubt I could ever find words to describe this place."

"It's one of my favorite parts of the estate. I come up here sometimes when I have trouble with an invention, or when I can't solve a problem. Something about the breeze and the sun and the view always clears my head."

"This place must be absolutely ferocious during a storm, though."

"It is. In fact, it's more than a little dangerous if the storm is heavy. Promise me you won't come up here alone in bad weather. Strike that—promise me you won't come up here alone at all, at least until we sort out your situation."

Sarah tilted her face up to the sun, grateful for the shelter Hartland's body provided. "It seems like such a small thing to agree to when you've sworn to protect my life."

"Nevertheless, I will have your word on this."

She breathed in a great lungful of sea air and let it out slowly. "I can't promise to always be an easy person to protect, but I will promise never to deliberately put myself in harm's way without consulting you first."

"You've been an Elliott less than a week, and already you sound like one of us." He loosened his arms and turned her around, brushing the hair away from her face when the wind blew it across her eyes. "But I'm serious about this. Even this far from London, you must be on your guard."

Her never-too-serious husband was frowning hard enough to put a crease just above the bridge of his nose, and she traced it with her forefinger. "I will be vigilant, Hartland. I swear."

He pushed her finger away and held her gaze for a long moment. Then he kissed her forehead and turned her to the magnificent view once more, wrapping his arms around her and holding her close. "Good."

"My lord, a messenger has arrived from London."

Hart looked up from the book of Latin poetry he'd been attempting to read to see his butler, Nichols, holding out a silver salver with a sealed letter. "The special messenger?"

"No, my lord. The one you left with Major Oliver."

Hart glanced over at Sarah in her now-customary place on the drawing room sofa, and forced himself to move at a normal pace as he accepted the letter. What he really wanted to do was tear the letter open and read it as fast as he could, but it wouldn't do to alarm his countess.

"Thank you, Nichols. See the messenger gets a meal and a bed for the night. I'll have a response for him to carry back to Town tomorrow."

Nichols bowed and left, and Hart broke the seal on the letter. He quickly scanned the pages of Ollie's utilitarian handwriting, hoping for information, for seeds of a plan to deal with the threat on Sarah's life.

What he found was like a punch to the gut.

The words were all jumbled as his eyes darted from one part of the page to the other, but he shifted his focus to a spot on the floor, took a breath, and tried again. Ollie wrote of some kind of attack in London, of bombs being detonated in a shop in Bond Street and some mysterious gas that filled the place. No one had been killed by the explosions, but the gas had an ill effect on many of those who'd been trapped in the shop. The perpetrator was unknown, and not likely to be discovered given the chaos that ensued.

He put a hand over his mouth, both to satisfy the urge to move and to keep himself from speaking. This was awful news in so many ways, but he decided not to concern Sarah with it—she already had enough to worry about.

Hart felt sick. There was no guarantee he would have been in that shop to stop the destruction, but it was likely he would have been nearby. And he would have been the lead horse in the pursuit that followed. He would have been there to track down the person that devised the attack and deliver him to the magistrate. He would have been there to see that the people caught in the shop received medical care, even if meant paying for it himself.

He would have been there to *do* something.

Balling up Ollie's letter, Hart squeezed it in one fist as hard as he could. Why had he been in such a hurry to leave London?

"Everything all right over there?"

Sarah's voice carried lightly across the room and Hart trained his gaze on her. There was no sun today, only a misty drizzle outside the large window, but she looked comfortable and content lying on the sofa with a book.

"Everything is fine," he replied, flashing her a smile. "Just a note from Ollie. Apparently a large number of ladies in Town have taken to their beds at the news of our marriage."

"Better than you taking to their beds."

He laughed. "Why Lady Hartland, you wound me."

She didn't look up from the page she was reading but he saw her lips curl into a small smile. "Do I?"

"No." He tossed the crumpled paper the length of the room so he didn't have to look at it. "I know my reputation."

Sarah closed the book over her thumb and turned her gaze on him. "But people are often more complex than mere reputations."

"Am I?"

"So far."

That pleased him more than he'd expected it to, and he felt his body relaxing slightly. Being able to temporarily push the shop bombing out of his mind helped, too. "I'll try not to disappoint you."

"You never have."

She picked up her book again and Hartland was thrown back into Ollie's letter, into that shop filled with explosions and noxious gas. Except he hadn't been there. And those people got hurt.

He'd done more than disappoint them. He'd left them unprotected.

There was a knock on the drawing room door and Nichols entered, once more bearing a silver tray with a sealed letter. "From the special messenger, my lord."

More information—wonderful. The more he knew, the better, and maybe this time it would be knowledge he could use. He plucked the letter from Nichols' tray and dismissed him, breaking the seal and unfolding the paper as fast as his fingers would move.

"Does 'special messenger' mean what I think it means?" Sarah asked from the sofa.

"You mean, does it have anything to do with your situation?" he returned, trying to keep his voice even.

She extended him the courtesy of several silent moments to read through the letter before prompting him. "Well?"

It was an account of the shop bombing, this time from Joanna Devlin—his Irish contact and the first member of Wellington's intelligence gathering ring—dated a day later than Ollie's. She had included a few details Ollie probably hadn't known, and confirmed the chaos at the scene. She also added a progress report on those that had been in the shop during the incident.

Three people have died so far, and a fourth will probably not last the night. But it wasn't the blasts that injured them, it was the gas that was contained inside the bombs. I spoke with one of the physicians who attended a victim, and he described his patient's symptoms as coughing and a burning sensation in the throat and eyes that progressed to nausea and vomiting. Then the lungs filled with fluid.

Hart cleared his throat. "Sorry, sweetheart. Nothing here about your admirer."

Her eyebrows drew together and her shoulders sagged, but Hart couldn't find the strength to try to make her smile. Three—probably four by now—people had died while Hart was hundreds of miles away taking a walk with his wife.

He rose in one swift motion and practically ran from the room. How could he sit there and continue to assure Sarah he would protect her when people were dying in London? How could he look her in the eyes when she was the reason he wasn't in Town?

He had just enough presence of mind to change into an older pair of trousers and worn shirt before heading out to his workshop. He had one at every home he owned, but the workshop at Hartland Abbey was particularly well-equipped. Between it and the forge next door, he could build practically anything. And while it was too late for the people who had already died, perhaps he could come up with a way to protect people the next time the bomber took his special toys out to play.

He had to.

"My lord, Lady Hartland sent me to ask if you will be taking your dinner here or in the dining room."

Hart looked up from the table he'd been hunched over to see his valet, Richards, standing before him. The light that had previously been pouring in through the arched windows had dwindled to a trickle, and Hart realized the sun had nearly sunk below the horizon.

He lit the lamp closest to him and looked around for another. "How long have I been out here?"

"About six hours."

Six hours, and all he had to show for it was a heap of failure. He'd been attempting to create a mask of sorts that would scrub impurities—like the shop bombing's mysterious gas—from the air and make it safe to breathe. But so far he'd only managed to create a pile of misshapen rubber and shattered glass.

"Did Lady Hartland say whether or not she preferred my company?"

"No, my lord."

"Has she asked about me in any capacity other than dinner arrangements?" Hart had commanded two of his burliest footmen to watch over her in his stead. Had she missed him at all?

"Not to me, but she could have asked Nichols or one of the other servants."

Would he be able to sit across from Sarah and act like nothing was wrong? Could he walk away from the mask before he had a working model? "Tell Lady Hartland I'll be in when I finish my work here."

"I'll have the kitchen prepare a tray for you."

Hart nodded and turned back to his worktable. If he was still there in the morning, Richards would also make arrangements for breakfast and clean clothing to be sent out. The footmen he'd set to guarding Sarah would remain with her until he gave them leave to return to their regular duties. Nothing else needed his specific attention, and he could go on working.

The door shut behind Richards and Hart sighed loudly, rubbing his eyes. At least this was a problem he had a chance of solving.

Chapter Seven

"Ah, Mr. Richards, there you are."

Hartland's valet turned and offered Sarah a smile as she entered the master's suite. His tall, spare form looked slightly out of place among the heavy, dark pieces of furniture, but he seemed perfectly at ease. "You have found me, my lady."

"Might I have a moment of your time?"

"Of course." He moved a pile of waistcoats from a chair and gestured for her to sit. "How may I be of service?"

She waited for him to clear a chair for himself, trying to decide how to phrase her question. When he was seated, she opted for directness over polite wording. "I'm worried about Hartland. You know him better than anyone else save perhaps Major Oliver. How does he look to you?"

Hartland had been out in his workshop for five straight days, not even returning to the house to sleep. Mrs. Nichols, the housekeeper, had warned Sarah not to go out there, that his lordship would only allow Richards to wait upon him when he was in this state. But after nearly a week of watching

Richards returning with barely-touched trays of food, she could no longer stand by and do nothing.

"He is..." Richards' voice trailed off as if he wasn't sure what to say.

"You may be blunt with me," she said gently. "I need to know the truth."

Richards cleared his throat. "He is not well, my lady. He's done this before, but I've never seen him this...this determined."

"Determined to do what?"

"To make his new invention work."

"Do you know what the invention is?"

Richards pursed his lips for a moment before answering. "He's trying to create some sort of mask, my lady. One that would allow the wearer to breathe easily even in the midst of smoke or other impurities in the air."

"A life-saving invention, I suspect." Then an idea dawned on her. "That's it, isn't it? He's driving himself so hard this time because the mask will save people's lives. He feels like he's actually accomplishing something." Unlike the days he spent reading in the drawing room with her.

"I believe so, my lady. But I do not know how much longer his body will stand up to the strain he is placing on it."

That was exactly what Sarah was afraid of. "Do you think he would rest if I went out and asked it of him?"

Sarah was Hartland's wife, and they'd had a moment or two that might be leading to a deeper affection. But no such attachment had developed between them as yet, and Sarah wasn't sure she held the necessary influence to pry an unwavering man from work he likely considered crucial.

To her surprise, Richards nodded. "He didn't pass along all the details, of course, but I know that he has made you promises beyond your marriage vows, my lady. Perhaps seeing you will remind him of his duty to you and make him more amenable to resting."

"That is precisely what I am hoping for."

Richards sat up straighter, as if his whole body was suddenly lighter. "I do hope you are successful."

"I shall do my very best." Sarah leaned forward and gave his hand a squeeze. Not the behavior of a countess toward a servant, but in this case she felt justified in making an exception. Mr. Richards was no ordinary servant and this was not a typical situation. "You have done a wonderful job taking care of him, Mr. Richards. I suspect he wouldn't be the man he is today without you."

The valet dropped his eyes to his shoes but smiled. "He is a good master."

Sarah rose and left Richards to his duties, visiting her own bedchamber and speaking to Lucy before heading down to the kitchen to put the next step of her plan in motion.

She was stopped midway by Nichols. "Lord Ashfield is here to see you, my lady."

"To see me?" The Ashfields lived several miles south of Hartland Abbey, and Lord Ashfield was the highest ranking aristocrat in the area after Hartland himself. Lord Ashfield was also rumored to be a man of science, as Mrs. Nichols had explained, so it wouldn't have been unusual for him to call upon Hartland. But to ask for the lady of the manor was distinctly odd, particularly since he'd never been introduced to her.

"Yes, my lady. He is waiting in the drawing room. Shall I tell him you are not at home?"

"No, I'll see him." Hartland certainly couldn't, not in his current state. And though it was unusual for Lord Ashfield to ask for Sarah, their meeting wasn't strictly prohibited either. "Thank you."

She smoothed her hair and skirts as she headed for the drawing room, thanking the heavens above that she hadn't yet changed to go out to Hartland's workshop. Stopping before the drawing room door, she took in a breath and let it out slowly.

He was standing when she entered the room, hands clasped behind his back, his forehead wrinkled in worry.

Sarah offered him her hand. "Good afternoon, Lord Ashford. To what do I owe this visit?"

He took her hand briefly and bowed over it, but straightened almost immediately. "I'd like to ask you some questions, Lady Hartland. If you don't object, of course."

"Questions about what?" She indicated the chair her husband frequently occupied and seated herself on the sofa.

"My wife." He sat in the offered chair, perched on the edge like a nervous bird. "She set out to call upon you two days ago and has not returned. Nor have her carriage and coachman been located."

Sarah sat up a little straighter. "Lady Ashfield has disappeared?"

"It appears so. How long was she here?"

"She wasn't here at all." Sarah's shoulders sagged under the weight of Lord Ashfield's palpable distress. "I didn't even know she was coming."

The wrinkles on his forehead drove his brows down over his eyes. "She wasn't, perhaps, in the village? Or the church next door? Could she have sent the coachman on an errand?"

Sarah shook her head. "I wouldn't know. I haven't been much beyond the boundaries of Hartland Abbey since I arrived. But I will ask our staff if any among them have seen her recently, and I'll send you a note when I have an answer."

"Thank you, Lady Hartland. I don't know what could have happened to her."

Sarah rose and escorted him to the door, wishing there was something more she could do to alleviate his concern. How awful to have his own wife disappear into thin air! "We must continue to hope that she is unharmed, Lord Ashfield. I will let you know what our servants report."

"Thank you," he said again, giving her a cursory bow.

Poor man. Sarah shook her head and resumed her journey to the kitchens, pausing to ask Mrs. Nichols to see to questioning the female staff. Mr. Nichols would handle the male servants, but if they turned up no information there was little else to be done.

She tried to push Lady Ashfield's disappearance —and Lord Ashfield's anxious face—from her mind. There was yet another person who needed help, and his was a situation in which she could offer assistance.

The kitchens at Hartland Abbey were immense compared to what Sarah had been accustomed to in London, and she'd thus far avoided the whole area. But she had a special purpose today. And when compared to marrying a near-stranger because her life was in danger, navigating the Hartland kitchens wasn't such a horror.

One of the kitchen maids, Becky, met her at the door and cheerfully complied with Sarah's request for luncheon items to take to Hartland. The maid found a basket of an appropriate size and headed for the larder, with Sarah trailing behind her.

"Sandwiches should please his lordship," Becky said almost to herself. She appropriated a loaf of bread, a large wedge of cheese, and a portion of ham, all of which she obligingly sliced and wrapped. "Some pickles, some early apples, pears….oh! And some late strawberries—they'll be delicious with the lemonade Cook made this morning." She added a plate of biscuits and some sort of pastry Sarah had never seen before, then packed it all neatly into the basket.

"What a wonderful meal," Sarah said, reaching for the basket with a smile. "I'm certain it will tempt his lordship out of his workshop for a while."

"I hope so, my lady. Judging by the trays he's sent back to the kitchen, he's hardly eaten a thing all week. Cook even made a special batch of meat pies she calls empanadas, his lordship's favorite."

He probably hadn't slept, either, if his tenacity about her own safety was any indicator. Sarah thanked Becky and promised to return for the basket, then hurried up to her chamber to change her gown. Richards' remark about her presence reminding Hartland of his duty to her had given her an idea. She thought perhaps if she wore an older gown, one Hartland had seen her in prior to their marriage, it might spark memories of her as a helpless maiden, which she knew was how he tended to think of her.

Lucy helped her mistress into the older gown and tidied her hair, but Sarah left off her bonnet and gloves. Hartland would be more able to connect with her if he could see her face, and the brim on the bonnet would all but prevent him from doing so. The gloves would be removed for eating, and Sarah saw little point in wearing them simply to take them off again. Once Lucy pronounced herself satisfied, Sarah armed herself with the picnic basket and headed for Hartland's workshop.

When she arrived, she set her basket down just outside the door and peered in. Hartland was standing before a stout table in his shirtsleeves, his dark hair matted down in some places and sticking up in others, molding a lump of some pliable substance with his bare hands. The lump tore in half without warning and Hartland roared unintelligibly. He shredded the substance and threw the pieces toward the far end of the big room.

"Why can't I make this work?" he yelled. "It has to work!"

Sarah had seen Hartland come into the bookshop bleary-eyed and wrung out time and time again, and she'd always assumed he'd been drinking and carousing. Occasionally he'd mentioned a days-long spree of inspiration and told her a little about what he'd been working on. In all cases he'd been in obvious need of rest and relaxation, but not like this. This was a side of Hartland she'd never seen before.

It was sheer raging mania.

Hart saw the shadow fall across the floor just inside the entrance of his workshop, but couldn't stop himself from flinging bits of rubber across the room as hard as he could. The substance tended to melt in warm weather and become brittle in the cold, but it was the best material he could think of to seal his mask. He had begun adding different things to the rubber sometime yesterday—he *thought* it was yesterday—in an effort to make it usable at all temperatures, but everything he'd tried so far had resulted in abject failure.

If he couldn't get the mask to work, more people would die. And it would be his fault.

"Hartland?"

Sarah's voice startled him into turning around. He'd been expecting his valet, not his wife.

He executed a clumsy bow. "At your service, my lady."

"Are you truly?"

"Yes, of course." Though whatever she wanted, he hoped it would be quick. He had work to do.

She smiled and pointed to an enormous basket just outside the doorway. "Then perhaps you'll help me dispose of this picnic luncheon."

"I can't stop. I have to figure this out."

"Hunger and fatigue cloud the mind," she replied, walking toward him and taking his hand. "Come outside with me and eat, just for a few minutes. Your head will be clearer for it."

She had a point there. He was so muzzy-headed he couldn't even remember which day it was. But his urge to keep going overruled her common sense. "I have to make this work."

"You're afraid if you stop, you'll lose valuable time. Something will happen that you could have prevented if you'd just worked for five minutes more."

How did she know that? Had she found Joanna's letter? "Perhaps."

She took his other hand in hers and stepped closer. "But right now, your actions are sluggish and your thoughts are muddled. You're like a farm horse that's been in the fields too long—tired and underperforming. But give the horse a rest, give him food and water, and the next day he's back to being strong and steady."

"I can't stop for a whole day—"

"Ten minutes," she said, interrupting his protestation. "Surely in ten minutes you can rest and eat. Fuel your brain as you would a fire, and it will burn more brightly."

A little food might help restore his focus. And Sarah might stop comparing him to animals and flames. "Ten minutes," he echoed, allowing her to lead him out of the workshop. "But only because you're prettier than anyone else who's come to see me this week."

She laughed and kissed his cheek, squeezing his hands and walking backwards to lead him from the workshop. "Mr. Richards is the only one who's been out here since you started this project."

"I know." On impulse, he released her hands and wrapped his arms around her waist. "You look much better in a dress than he does."

"When has Mr. Richards ever worn a dress?"

"It's a long story—one you probably don't want to hear."

"I'll take your word for it."

He studied her face as the warmth of her hands seeped through his linen shirt. Hart couldn't pinpoint why, but somehow it was important that his wife think well of him. He couldn't tell her about the intelligence gathering ring and his work for Wellington, nor would she want to hear the ugly details of the shop bombing in London and the mysterious gas he was trying to save people from.

But he could tell her his own personal secrets. "I know you think I'm some sort of profligate rakehell, but I'm actually not."

"No?" She was still smiling, but her eyes were trained on his and she cinched her arms more tightly around his shoulders. "Then what are you?"

"I'm no angel, either. I don't deny that I like gambling and drinking, or that I find most people boring beyond reason and treat them as nuisances. But I'm not the womanizer you think I am."

Her smile faded and was replaced by raised eyebrows. "Are you not?"

"No. I play the game in public, smile and flirt and make lewd innuendos. It's expected of me. I've had my share of mistresses, too. But... I think what I'm trying to say is that I'm not as wicked as my reputation might lead you to believe."

"My mother will be relieved to hear that."

"What about you?" he asked with an earnest note in his voice he wished wasn't there. He was starting to sound like a schoolboy begging for approval.

Sarah tilted her head slightly to one side, as if she was contemplating a great mystery of the universe, then feathered her fingers through the hair at his temple. "I know how you've treated me, your servants, and your friend. That's empirical evidence. Everyone else's opinion is just theory."

"And what does your evidence tell you?"

"That you are every inch an aristocrat who thinks himself above most of the people in the world." Her smile returned. "And that you have a bigger heart and sense of honor than you're willing to admit."

Hart's whole body relaxed. "Are you sure you're not biased? I am in the process of saving your life, after all."

"You won't be saving anyone if you don't eat." She kissed his other cheek and pulled away from him. "Come on."

The sun was so harsh Hart could barely open his eyes when he followed Sarah out of the workshop, but he managed to help her spread out a blanket in the grass near the stream. They sorted through the items in the basket next, and he realized this was the picnic—no servants, no table and chairs, no formal place settings, just Hart and his wife on a blanket.

"How did you carry this basket all the way out here?" Out of habit, he'd insisted on carrying the basket the short distance to their picnic site. The thing felt like it was full of rocks.

Sarah laughed. "I've been carrying stacks of books since I was old enough to read them. Do you know how much Johnson's *A Dictionary of the English Language* weighs?"

"I never thought about it before." He briefly wondered if she was strong enough to swing the big hammers he kept in the forge and was seized by a vision of his wife working a piece of steel at the anvil. It was disconcerting and intriguing all at once.

"Nichols says you've received another letter from the special messenger," Sarah told him, pulling him from his musings. She'd set out their main course and began assembling a sandwich from the various components. "And I have news from Lord Ashfield."

At the smell of the sliced ham and cheese, his stomach awakened with a rumble. He built his own sandwich and took a big bite. "What letter? What news?"

"I brought the letter with me. Nichols seemed to think it was important."

"It is. Where is it?"

She snatched the basket and moved it to the other side of the blanket. "Not until you finish eating."

"Very well, my lady. What shall we talk about, then?"

"Tell me about your invention—the one you're currently working on."

He supposed it wouldn't hurt to tell her what he was trying to create. He'd just keep the inspiration for the device to himself. "Know anything about making dirty air cleaner?"

"I might. What are you trying to do?"

He'd been joking about her possible knowledge of filtering air, but she answered in a serious tone. Well, maybe she could help him make a connection he was missing. "I'm building a mask that a person could wear when the air is not breathable. It will be made from sturdy leather, with slits through which air will be drawn in. I want to use rubber to form a seal around the glass eyeholes—that's what I was attempting to do when you walked in—and I need something to scrub the air, as it were, before it is inhaled."

Sarah popped a piece of cheese into her mouth and chewed. "What about charcoal?" she asked when she'd swallowed.

"Charcoal?"

"Indeed. It's used to remove the color and impurities from sugar syrup so the final product is white. And there was a scientist in Russia who used it to filter his vodka. He reported that the vodka tasted smoother and cleaner after it had been passed through a layer of powdered charcoal."

Well, well ,well, it seemed he'd underestimated his countess's academic prowess. "How do you know that?"

She flashed him a grin. "Remember all those books I carried? I read every single one."

"Including chemistry texts, as it turns out. I'm surprised your father allowed that."

"Papa encouraged me to read everything. He said the more familiar I was with the books we stocked, the better able I would be to help customers find what they wanted and give them recommendations."

"Good business sense." He accepted the cup of lemonade she poured for him and used it to wash down the rest of his sandwich. "Wait a minute, is that why you suggested Davy's paper to me when I came in to the bookshop that last time? Because you're interested in chemistry?"

A dimple appeared in her cheek as she tried unsuccessfully to suppress another smile. "I may also have been trying to get you interested in the subject."

"You didn't think I read enough science texts?"

"I thought your library would benefit from the addition of a different science. Yours is mostly physics and metallurgy." She put the cup down and dropped her eyes to her hands. "I may also have been conducting a little experiment."

Oh? "What kind of experiment?"

"I wanted to see what you'd say to me, what you'd ask me about a chemistry text."

"And how did I do?"

She busied herself rummaging in the basket and came up with a plate of pastries. "Better than most. You asked my opinion of the paper and actually listened to my answer."

"Isn't that the way people are supposed to act with one another?" He took a pastry from the plate she'd placed between them and bit into it, closing his eyes for a brief moment in sheer bliss. He would have to thank Joanna—again—for talking him in to hiring this cook. "I'm not exactly an expert on social interaction, though."

Sarah's eyes followed his hand as it lifted the pastry to his mouth again, but he got the feeling she wasn't really focused on him. "The ladies that came into the shop were mostly attentive when I answered their questions. But our gentlemen customers preferred to deal with Mr. Higgins."

"Surly they didn't spurn your help for his."

"Not outright, no. And not usually when it came to books they were purchasing for a woman. But for physics, chemistry, anatomy... Well, those subjects are too advanced for a lady to comprehend..."

Her voice trailed off, and Hart felt his heart beat faster even as he struggled to stay awake. "Higgins doesn't know anything about physics or anatomy, or probably chemistry either. He once tried to explain to me how the human heart functioned, and somehow managed to make mention of meteors and comets in the telling."

Sarah chose a pastry from the plate and tore off a small piece. "How on earth did he do that?"

"I have no idea. I was so confused by the time he was done, I wasn't even sure what we were discussing anymore."

"Higgins isn't a bad sort, though. He was the man to see when it came to poetry." She began shredding the pastry, producing crumbs on the section of blanket before her. "I hope he will be able to find other employment."

Hart polished off his own pastry in three bites and stretched out on his back. "He already did."

"Doing what?"

"Cataloging and maintaining Preston's personal library. Lords have a tendency to accumulate books without reading them, and Preston's collection was a complete mystery to him."

"Preston didn't even know Mr. Higgins existed. How did they find each other?

Hart finally gave in and closed his eyes. "I might have made an introduction."

He heard the gentle swish of fabric just before soft lips caressed his. When Sarah drew back, Hart opened his eyes to find her kneeling beside him. "What was that for? Not that I'm complaining. I want to know what it was so I can do it again."

She laughed and his heartbeat picked up speed once more, but for an entirely different reason. "You have saved a life, Hartland—or rather, four lives. Mr. Higgins has a wife and two children to support, which he will continue to do thanks to you."

"Save a life, get a kiss?" he grinned. "Can we make that a permanent agreement?"

"Yes," she answered, leaning down again. "In fact, let's make it two kisses."

This time he was ready for her, and wrapped her in his arms when her lips met his. She was soft and welcoming and enthusiastic, and he was glad he'd let Richards badger him into cleaning his teeth that morning. He drew her down to the blanket and raised himself over her on one elbow, threading his fingers through her hair and dislodging every pin he came in contact with. Her arms came around his shoulders, hands running down his back then under the hem of his untucked shirt. The pads of her fingers glided across his skin and his breathing hitched. He'd been with other women before, of course, done things with them that were much more intimate, but this felt different somehow. He recognized the lust rising in his body, but it was mixed with something else he couldn't quite name.

Whatever it was, he was enjoying himself enormously and so, by the feel of her, was Sarah. It almost made him regret the deal he'd made with her lady's maid.

"I'd better get back to work, then," he said, breaking the kiss—and the moment. He couldn't continue such an intimate act while thinking about that deal. And he needed to get back to his mask. "I have a lot of lives to save."

Hart started to sit up but Sarah turned the tables on him, levering herself above him and pushing him back down onto the blanket. "Not yet. Food and rest is what we agreed on, and you haven't yet had any rest."

"A few minutes is what we agreed on," he reminded her, not quite recalling the exact number she'd used. "And it's been far longer than that already."

"What can I do to convince you to sleep?"

He thought that one over for a moment and blurted out the only answer that came into his mind. "You could sleep with me."

She flushed pink at his double entendre but kept her hands on his chest. "Would you like that?"

"Very much." His fingers skimmed her bare arms and he watched a shiver follow in their wake. The urge to follow that shiver with his lips was strong, but his tired body would not comply. "Would you?"

For a long moment she just looked at him, eyes the color of the Devon sky set in an unreadable mask. Then her swollen, eminently kissable lips curved into a smile. "Yes, I think I would." She laid down beside him, resting her head on his shoulder and her hand inside the opening of his shirt. "But if you'd rather I stayed awake while you slept, I can do that, too."

He laughed and embraced her, kissing her forehead. "Whatever you think is best, my lady. I am in your hands."

Chapter Eight

"Excellent, my lord. You nearly took me to the ground that time."

Hart grinned at his valet, standing opposite him in the clearing near the workshop. Both men were clothed in trousers and shirts, sleeves rolled above their elbows with matching sweat stains spreading across their backs.

"If you weren't so wily, Richards, there would have been no 'nearly.'"

"If one is fighting for one's life, being 'wily' is often helpful."

Hart wiped his forehead with his sleeve and planted his feet. "Let's go again."

Richards took up his stance and made to rush his master when a feminine voice called out, "Is this how the two of you work up an appetite?"

Both men turned as Sarah approached, a blanket thrown over one arm and a basket presumably full of food on the other. It had been several days since her initial picnic with Hart in the midst of his week-long compulsion to work, and Sarah had continued to bring a midday meal out to his workshop. He thought perhaps it settled her mind to see him eat and to inspect his appearance for signs of neglect. And he liked having her all to himself, even if it was only for twenty minutes.

"I needed the practice," Hart returned in answer to her question. "Haven't done a lot of fighting since we arrived. But now that you mention it, I'm starving."

Richards bowed politely and began to excuse himself, but Sarah stopped him. "You were fighting?"

"Training," Richards supplied. "To keep ready in case..."

In case a killer came calling. Neither man said it aloud, but Sarah gave a little nod as if she understood and turned her eyes on her husband. "Do you think I should learn to fight?"

"No need, my lady. You have me, Richards, and the entire male population of Hartland Abbey to keep you safe."

She lowered her basket to the ground and dropped the blanket atop it. "Isn't it possible, though, that I might be caught unawares and out of the sight of all Hartland males?"

However unlikely on Hart's own property, it *was* possible. Since the disappearance of Lady

Ashfield and the recent recovery of her abandoned carriage twenty miles from Hartland, he'd had more than one nightmare in which Sarah simply vanished despite the vigilance of her husband and impromptu guard.

He must have been giving her a strange look because she continued, "Wouldn't it make sense for me to be able to defend myself under those circumstances?"

"Lady Hartland has a point, my lord," Richards put in. "It never hurts to be prepared, no matter how improbable a situation may seem."

"Think of it as another way to protect me," she added, stepping closer to Hartland and smiling softly. "Knowledge is a powerful tool. And if you share some of your knowledge with me, it will be as if you're there with me, even when you're not."

That clinched it. His feelings on the subject went from skeptical to acquiescent in a matter of seconds. Hart knew he couldn't leave his hunted wife without every possible means of protection. "Fine. Richards, you are dismissed. I'll instruct her ladyship myself."

Richards obeyed and Sarah shed the bonnet she'd worn, dropping it on the ground beside the picnic basket. Hart closed the distance between them and placed himself directly in front of her.

"Your objective is to simply get away. Once your attacker has released you, you run like hell to me, to Richards, or to the nearest populated area. Understand?"

She nodded solemnly. "Yes."

"If he comes at you from the front, your best option is a well-placed knee." Her brows drew together as if she was working out the mechanics of the move, and he laughed. "Put your hands on my shoulders. Notice how close we are? If you raised your knee with any sort of force…"

Sarah looked down at her knees and chuckled. "Yes, I can see how that would encourage my release."

"If you aren't in a position to use your knee, bend back his first two fingers as far as you can make them go." He retrieved one of her hands from his shoulder and grasped her index and middle fingers, gently pushing them away from her palm. "Feel that?"

"I do. Can I try on you?"

"Certainly."

He offered his right hand and she closed hers around his wrist, taking his two fingers in her left.

"The closer you get to the base of the fingers, the more you'll pull on the long tendons," he said, his eyes never leaving their joined hands.

Sarah slid her hand down as far as it would go and pulled his fingers toward the back of his hand. "Like this?"

"Mmhmm, just like that." The tendons in his wrist became tight, and he could feel pain and pressure all the way down his forearm. Hartland tried to lower his hand to ease the discomfort, but she held him fast. "It doesn't take much, sweetheart."

She flashed him a smile and let go. "No, it doesn't. That's what makes it useful, isn't it?"

"Exactly." He took Sarah by the shoulders and turned her away from him, flexing his fingers when he was certain she couldn't see him do it. "Now, if he grabs you from behind, there are a couple of things you can do." He wrapped his arms around her, inhaling the scent of the delicate, lemony perfume she wore and resisting the urge to trail kisses down the side of her neck. "First, stomp on his foot as hard as you can."

Sarah laughed again. "Surely you don't expect me to do that to you."

"No, but you should practice the movement."

She obliged and brought her foot down upon Hart's with what was probably half the force she was capable of.

"That may be enough to get your assailant to release you. If it's not, it's almost guaranteed to get him to lean forward…" He demonstrated, bending at the waist as if she'd caused real pain to his foot. "…and you can elbow him in the nose."

He grasped her elbow and guided it backward toward his face. The contact between their bare limbs momentarily distracted him, filling his thoughts with other ways they could be skin to skin.

"In the nose? Isn't that a rather small target to aim for?"

He gave himself a mental shake. "Yes, but if you hit it you'll disable your attacker instantly, even if you don't break it. If you miss, you're still likely to hit a cheekbone or an eye socket, and that can cause enough pain for your attacker to lose his focus on you. Try it."

She dutifully swung her elbow backward and made contact with his nose—barely a tap, but Hart let out a yowl and covered his face with both hands. Sarah's hands were on his shoulders in seconds.

"Oh, Hart! Are you all right? I'm so sorry!" Her fingers caressed his temples, then slid over his hands. "How bad is it? Let me see…"

He dropped his hands from his face and wrapped her in his arms. "You're supposed to run away, my lady."

She stared at him for a moment, motionless. Then her hands clamped down on his shoulders. "Andrew Elliott, don't you ever scare me like that again!"

"I'm sorry," Hart said, trying to stifle the laughter that threatened to erupt. "I only wanted to see your reaction. I didn't mean to frighten you."

"Would you find it funny if I made you believe you'd hurt me?"

Her voice was controlled, but that made her words all the more sharp. How *would* he react if he thought he'd hurt her?

"I wouldn't find it funny at all. I am sworn to protect you, not hurt you."

Her body relaxed in his arms. "I'm glad to hear it. Now, will you go and wash? You're dripping sweat all over my gown."

He placed a big smacking kiss on her cheek and took himself off to the stream. "I shall return posthaste."

By the time he made his way back to her, his dark hair curling riotously as it dried, she'd unpacked their luncheon and arranged it on the blanket. He ignored the food and plopped down beside her.

"Better?" he asked, leaning toward her.

She took the opportunity to stroke his hair, his cheek. He did look better, and not just because of his impromptu bath. Richards only managed to persuade Hartland to shave every few days, and his eyes were red-rimmed after too many nights with too little sleep. The desire and drive to succeed still burned brightly in his brown eyes, but the mania seemed to have subsided. "Much."

He held her gaze for several moments, then took her hand from his face and placed a kiss on her palm. "Good. Is there anything else you require of me before we eat?"

Fat drops of rain began to splash on Sarah's arms and hair. "Perhaps a dry place for our meal?"

They rushed to repack the basket as the frequency of the drops increased, dashing into the workshop just the sky opened up.

"Are you very wet?" Hartland asked, setting the basket down in front of one of the floor-to-ceiling windows.

"A little damp around the edges, but that's all. You?"

"I still hadn't completely dried from my bath," he grinned.

She draped the blanket around his shoulders and patted his face dry with one corner. "No harm done, then."

"Sit," he offered, pulling a chair from one sturdy, scarred wooden table and removing a box of tools from it. "Rest a moment."

Sarah complied, but not for much longer than Hartland's suggested moment. His workshop was a cornucopia of tools, scientific instruments, and related accoutrements. One table contained nothing but metal plates of various shapes and sizes. "Are those pieces of armor?" she asked, rising from the chair and drifting toward the table.

"Yes." He dropped the blanket and arrived at the table before she did, picking up random pieces and putting them down as he went.

"These plates are so small. How do they protect you?" She ran a finger over a rectangular piece smaller than her hand.

"That is from one of my brigandines." He pulled a large black garment from the table and held it up. It looked like a long, thick waistcoat but was covered in rivets and had buckles along the front instead of buttons. "These little plates are attached to layers of canvas, like this..."

He turned out one side of the garment, revealing dozens of plates similar to the one on the table arranged in overlapping rows.

"How clever," she smiled. "Much more portable than a suit of plate armor."

"Exactly. And this is easier to move in." He donned the brigandine and buckled it closed, then proceeded to twist and turn. "See? I can even dance in it."

He swept her into his arms and began waltzing her around the room, dodging tables and stools and boxes as they went. Sarah let herself get caught up in the moment, dancing with her dashing husband. Never mind that he'd only married her because someone wanted her dead, or that they'd planned to live separate lives once she was safe again. They were dancing together to the rhythm of the rainfall as it pelted the windows, and there was no one in the world but the two of them.

When he brought them to a halt beside the table of armor she flattened her palms against his broad chest. "I can feel the plates underneath. Don't they hurt you?"

He covered her hands with his and held them in place over his heart. "I usually wear a padded leather coat underneath. That keeps the plates from causing damage and serves as another layer of protection."

"Good thinking."

"Would that I could take credit for it." He twirled her around by the hand, then slid his arm around her waist. "It's a medieval concept, I've just made some improvements."

"Such as?"

"I used a different method to make the steel so it's stronger than what they had, for one thing."

Her eyes dropped to the pattern of rivets and she poked one with her index finger. "Strong enough to stop a bullet?" When he didn't answer, she raised her eyes to his. "I'll take that as a 'no' then."

Hartland shook his head. "Strong enough to stop a blade and most flying debris. And this black layer is wool, which is safer in a fire than other fabrics."

In a fire? "Do you often run into burning buildings?"

"It's been known to happen."

Sarah made a mental note to find her favorite chemistry text and see if she couldn't come up with something better than plain wool. He was protecting her from a killer, after all. The least she could do was help protect him from fire.

"What made you decide to build armor and fight crime?" The question had been percolating in her mind for some time. Standing before the man himself while he was wearing said armor seemed liked a good time to ask.

He loosened his arm about her waist. "Why do we always talk about me? Why do we never talk about you?"

If he was deflecting, his answer was either embarrassing or very personal. Sarah filed that tidbit away for later and allowed him to change the subject. "What would you like to know?"

"Your favorite color."

Of all the questions he could ask her, he chose to ask about her favorite color? "Green, I think."

"Is that why you wore a green dress for our wedding?"

Her eyes widened. She hadn't expected him to remember a detail like that. "I suppose so, though not directly. I'd had that one made for Diana's ball, and chose the green because it was my favorite. When we were wed, I wanted to wear my best gown and that one was it."

"That makes sense. What about pastimes? What do you do for fun?" He cinched his arms more tightly about her waist. "Other than read books, I mean. I already know about that."

"I embroider, of course, and I knit on occasion, though my mother would be horrified if she discovered that."

He laughed. "Why on earth is knitting so awful?"

"Ladies of quality don't, as a rule, knit. I think it's too practical. A knitter creates a useful item that no longer has to be purchased and isn't as fine as one might find in a shop."

"You've thought this through, haven't you?" His eyes crinkled up at the corners as his smile grew. He didn't appear to be mocking her, though, just enjoying this glimpse into her mind.

"I have." She grinned up at him. "What's the point in doing something in defiance of popular expectations if you don't think it through?"

"I do things in defiance of popular expectations all the time, you know. Mostly because they're fun."

"Things like marry a woman whose father was a merchant?" she asked, beginning to lose enthusiasm for the conversation. "That hasn't exactly been fun."

He stroked her hair gently, and caressed her cheek. "Fun is perhaps the wrong word for what we've been doing. But we're managing well enough, aren't we?"

"I am alive and uninjured, so that part is going well so far." She slid her hands up his arms and rested them on his shoulders. "And we seem to be getting along rather nicely, too."

"Now if we can just figure out who is causing you all this trouble, we can improve your situation even further."

He said it with a note of bitterness hiding among the optimism. She wrapped her arms around his neck and lay her cheek against his. If she was safe anywhere, it was here in the Armored Man's arms in his own workshop. "I know you'd rather be in Town figuring out who's behind this. I'm sorry you're stuck out here with me."

He drew back and looked her straight in the eye. "I would like to be in the thick of things—that much is true. But I'm not sorry I brought you here. Hartland Abbey is where you're safe, and that means more to me than any fight."

He kissed her then, with an intensity that surprised her. But she had little time to contemplate his motive before the pure pleasure of his mouth on hers washed all other thoughts from her mind.

Chapter Nine

IT WAS SEVERAL hours before Sarah could concentrate on anything except kissing Hart. He wasn't the first man to kiss her, or even the second. But her relationship with Hartland was different than anything she'd had with anyone else. Part of that was due to their marriage, certainly, but Sarah had known plenty of married couples who treated each other like polite strangers. Part of the interest he showed her was also no doubt due to the threat that had been issued against her, but that didn't explain the tender way he touched her or the ardor in his kisses.

And it didn't explain why her heart pounded whenever he was near.

Eventually she settled in at the escritoire in her bedchamber to write a letter to her mother, to be carried north by one of Hartland's personal messengers. Lucy bustled about, putting away clean frocks and removing soiled items for further attention, and Sarah found the maid's quiet activity helped her concentrate. It wasn't too long before she was lost in her letter, trying to describe the magnificence of the Devon coast.

"Sarah, are you in here?"

Hartland's voice drifted in from her dressing room. She set her pen carefully on the blotter and went to meet him. "Yes, I'm here."

He emerged from her dressing room dressed in neatly pressed trousers, a clean shirt, starched cravat, and an exquisitely tailored navy blue waistcoat. It was the most clothing she'd seen on him since they'd arrived at Hartland Abbey, and it was all immaculate.

"Good. Are you busy? Do you have a moment to talk?" His voice was light but he wouldn't make eye contact with her for more than two seconds at a time.

"I have plenty of moments. What would you like to discuss?"

He shifted his weight from one foot to the other. "There's something I need to—"

Lucy popped in through the chamber door at the other end of the room with an armload of gowns. "Alright, my lady, this should be the last bunch, then I'll just..." Her voice died away. "I'm sorry, my lady, I didn't realize—"

"It's fine, Lucy. I told you to come and go as you needed," Sarah said.

Lucy glanced at Hartland before returning her gaze to her mistress. "I'll just go. I can take care of these later."

"It's all right. His lordship and I were only talking. Finish what you need to finish and then you may go."

"My lord, Mr. Richards was looking for you the last time I was downstairs. He said something about a special messenger arriving."

"Thank you. I'll speak with him directly."

Lucy curtsied, throwing another glance at Hartland, then Sarah, before disappearing into Sarah's dressing room with the gowns.

What was that about? Not all that long ago Hartland had insisted he wasn't as wicked as his reputation suggested, but he was clearly involved in something with Lucy. Had he lied to Sarah about his relationship with other women or was there something else going on between her husband and her maid?

Lucy closed the dressing room door behind her and Sarah turned her gaze on Hartland. "What were you saying?"

"That...Nichols told me we received an invitation this afternoon. You are the mistress of the house and in charge of our social matters, but Nichols is used to informing me of such things."

She was certain that wasn't what Hartland had originally come to say, but they had indeed received an invitation from their nearest aristocratic neighbor. She ushered him into her chamber and seated herself at her escritoire, gesturing him to take a nearby chair. "The Wiltons have asked us to join them for dinner."

"Do you want to go?"

That was a question Sarah had asked herself all afternoon. Having been confined to the estate from the moment she arrived, she was growing curious about the neighbors and the area. And yet, she was reluctant to allow the world outside Hartland Abbey to intrude on the quiet life she'd been living with her husband.

"I think so. Do you?"

"No. The Wiltons are perfectly nice people, but they bore me."

Sarah felt her mouth curving into a smile. "Everyone bores you."

"You don't."

High praise indeed. But in light of his mysterious collusion with Lucy, she elected to ignore the implication. "Then perhaps you can think of it as an evening spent with me. There will just be two other people there with us."

"It's not a dinner party?"

She shook her head. "Mrs. Wilton's note said we were the only ones invited."

"That makes security easier."

Lest she forget someone wanted her dead. "Surely you don't mean to summon an army for a few miles' drive?"

"The safest thing to do would be to stay home," he replied, setting his hands on his knees. "But if you want to accept this dinner invitation, summoning an army is one way to ensure your safety."

"Or there's the quiet approach: unmarked carriage, one or two armed guards, garner as little notice as possible. Like we did on the way here."

Hartland nodded. "The head coachman is a trained fighter, and Richards could accompany us."

"Richards?"

He leaned back in his chair. "He spent twenty years with His Majesty's Army, mostly in North America."

That explained Richards' sparring session with his master. He didn't just look after Hartland's clothing, he saw to Hartland's physical training as well. "So he can handle himself if we're..."

She couldn't bring herself to say the word *attacked*, but Hartland nodded again. "Richards is a good man to have around when things get dangerous."

"We don't have to go," Sarah offered. Even if Hartland didn't call out the entire county to protect her, the whole undertaking was beginning to sound like a lot of effort for a simple dinner. "We're still newly wed and no one would begrudge us this time alone together."

"You mean we can turn down the invitation with no social consequences." He flashed her a smile and slid down a little in his chair. "You ought to know me well enough by now to know I don't care about social consequences."

"I know you don't, but in this case we have a graceful way out if we want it."

Hartland folded his hands over his stomach. "No, we can go. It will do us both some good, I think, to have a little change of scenery."

"Even if the Wiltons are boring?"

He grinned. "Even if the Wiltons are boring. The food is bound to be good, and I will have several minutes alone with you in a dark carriage."

Sarah's lips curved into a smile before she could stop them. Alone in the dark with her husband would almost certainly be more pleasurable than dining with the Wiltons, yet she couldn't help but tease him a little. "Just enough time for a short nap."

"If that's what you want to call it." He winked and rose, taking both her hands in his and kissing each one in turn. "Tell Mrs. Wilton we'll be there. I'll make the arrangements."

"I will send her a reply tomorrow."

Sarah watched her husband exit her bedchamber through the dressing room, passing Lucy with no more than a cursory acknowledgment as she headed for her mistress. Lucy wasn't as circumspect in her reaction, however, and stared as Hartland went by her, dropping her eyes to her shoes when gave her a nod.

Time to find out what was going on between them. "Lucy, did you overhear what Lord Hartland and I were discussing?"

"I tried not to, my lady..."

"You aren't in any trouble," Sarah said, hoping to reassure the girl. "I only wanted to be sure you knew about our dinner with Mr. and Mrs. Wilton.

You will finally be able to put your skills to real use instead of dressing me simply to haunt this old house.”

“Of course, my lady. I would be pleased to do whatever you need.”

“Wonderful. If you’re finished with my wardrobe for the evening, there is one more thing you can help me with. Or perhaps it is something I can help you with.”

Lucy’s brows drew together. “I don’t understand. What can you help me with?”

“A situation you might be in that you feel you can’t escape from.”

“My lady?”

“Have you been receiving unwanted attention from any of the men here?”

Lucy’s expression lightened. “Oh no, my lady. His lordship does not tolerate that sort of thing. If he finds out one of the male staff tried to make unwanted advances on a female servant, he dismisses the offending male.”

“Really?” It was usually the female servant who was dismissed, because she was a “temptation” or “distraction” to the men.

“Yes, my lady. His lordship says he has a hard enough time behaving properly himself, that he needs his staff to look after him not the other way 'round. Female servants have been dismissed, too, of course, when they get with child or what have you. But if one of the footmen had his eye on me, Mr. Nichols or his lordship would take care of it."

"That's a relief." But what if Hartland was the one who had his eye on a maid? "So you're not having difficulties here?"

"No, my lady." Lucy smiled cheerfully. "Doing for you is the best situation I've had yet."

"Well that's good to hear."

"Do you need anything else this evening?"

Sarah pushed herself out of her chair. "Just to help me out of this gown."

Lucy had her mistress out of her gown and into a wrapper in a few minutes, carefully tending to the discarded clothing before curtsying and heading for the chamber door.

"Lucy?"

"Yes, my lady?"

"You would tell me if you did have difficulties, wouldn't you?"

"Of course I would."

Sarah paused, but added one more question. "Even if his lordship was the cause?"

Lucy's shoulders slumped, but her expression remained neutral. "Even then."

Dinner with the Wiltons turned out to be everything Hart had predicted: the food was good, the Wiltons were boring, and the short drive home was spent with his wife in a darkened carriage. Sarah seemed somewhat absent, though, as they wound their way through the countryside. She rested her head on his shoulder when he drew her against him, but there were none of her caresses or sighs, no teasing, no questioning, just...silence.

Was she worried about her safety? Thinking of her mother? Remembering the lovely strawberry tart they'd had for dessert?

"You're awfully quiet, my lady."

"Just tired," she replied softly. "I'd forgotten how much work it is to socialize with strangers."

The carriage came to a halt just as they'd begun to descend into the valley that surrounded Hartland Abbey. Hart looked down at Sarah, then out the window.

"Why did we stop?" she asked, sitting up.

He shook his head slightly. "I don't know."

A moment later the carriage door opened and Richards stuck his head inside. "My apologies, my lord. A tree has fallen across the road and we can't get the carriage around it. It will probably take us some time to make the road passable again."

And in the meantime, Hart and Sarah would be easy targets in the carriage. "Very well. I'll escort her ladyship to the house on foot while the two of you deal with this. If we take one of the lanterns, can you work by just the other?"

"Yes, my lord. The moon is bright enough to see by tonight."

"Good. That's what we'll do, then."

As Richards nodded and closed the door, Hart opened up the storage area underneath the rear-facing seat. When he returned to his own seat he was holding a brigandine similar to the one he'd shown her in his workshop a few days ago. This one was royal blue and would be ill-fitting on a woman, but it was better than nothing.

"I want you to put this on," he told her, holding it open wide enough for her to slip her arms in. "It's just a precaution, but it will make me feel better to have you in it."

He couldn't see her eyes in the dark, but her voice was steady when she spoke. "What if you need it?"

"I'll be fine for the walk up to the house." A heavy silence followed and he felt compelled to add, "I don't think we'll have any trouble, but I've fought before without my armor. If I need to tonight, I can."

She laid her hand on his cheek for a couple of heartbeats without speaking but eventually complied, allowing him to drape the brigandine around her body and fasten the buckles down the front.

"Ready?" he asked. The question was directed to Sarah, but he suspected it was also meant for himself.

"Ready."

He exited the carriage first then handed her down, drawing her arm through his and holding the lantern out before them. "Just a quiet walk on a lovely September night."

"After a less-than-stimulating evening with the neighbors," she finished, laying her head on his shoulder once more. She dropped her voice to nearly a whisper and asked, "Why are you so concerned tonight?"

He released her arm and slid his around her waist. "There hasn't been a storm strong enough to topple a tree since we've been here," he murmured.

"So how did the tree fall across the road?"

"Exactly."

She covered his hand at her waist with her cold fingers but didn't reply. They simply continued their steady walk toward the Abbey in silence.

About halfway down the road Hart heard footsteps crunching softly behind them. But before he could even turn his head to locate the source of the noise, Sarah was ripped from him and disappeared into the darkness.

Then he heard her screaming.

"Sarah!"

He felt the hard tip of a knife pressed against his back. "Move and I'll gut you like a fish."

He slowly raised his hands to shoulder height, palms out to show he wasn't armed. "Just because you have a fish on your line doesn't mean you'll eat it for dinner."

"What?"

Hart whirled around, kicking his leg out and using his momentum to take out his assailant's knee. The crack of splintering bone hit Hart's ears like a hammer on one of his anvils, and the lantern hit the ground and extinguished itself. The assailant dropped to one knee but swung his arm out, wildly slashing the air with his knife. Sarah's screams had grown more frantic and Hart's pulse raced. Nothing was more important than getting to her. He dodged the blade and got in close, landing a solid punch to the assailant's face. The man landed on his back in the middle of the road but continued flailing. Hart couldn't tell if the man was trying to rise or to injure his quarry from where he lay, but he didn't have time to find out. Stepping on his attacker's wrist convinced the man to drop the knife, and Hart grabbed it up as he charged toward Sarah's voice.

A second attacker had wrapped her in his arms from behind, not all that differently from Hart's own demonstration just days earlier. This time, though, his countess was thrashing about as she screamed, attempting to avoid the knife her attacker wielded. Hart's heart nearly stopped when it sliced Sarah's flailing arm, but his legs continued pumping as fast as he could make them.

When he was only a few yards away Sarah threw her head back, bashing her attacker in the face. Hart didn't have to hear the squishing crunch to know she'd broken the man's nose—the blood that poured out coupled with the attacker's own scream said that clearly enough. He doubled over in pain, face in his hands, and Sarah ran.

"I'm here, sweetheart," Hart called, reaching for her as she came toward him. "I'm here, and you're safe."

She flung her arms around him and held him tightly even as her body shook from fear and exertion. She didn't speak, only buried her face against his neck.

"There now, my love. I've got you." He stroked her hair where it had tumbled from its pins and murmured the words over and over, desperately wishing he could do more to ease her panic.

But her breathing eventually reached a less frenzied pace, and she raised her face. "Is he dead?"

Hart hadn't even noticed that her attacker had gone quiet, and peered around his wife to get a look. "I don't think so. I can't tell from here if he's still breathing. He may have simply fainted from the pain of his injury. Do you want me to go and check?"

"No." She tightened her arms around him and dropped her forehead to his shoulder. "Not yet. Will you just hold me for a few more minutes?"

"I'll hold you forever if you want me to."

She let out a heavy sigh. "Good."

What seemed like hours later—but was probably only a minute or two—Richards ran up with the coachman on his heels.

"My lord! Are you all right? We heard screaming..."

"We are both unharmed, more or less. Would you be so kind as to secure our two guests and provide them with accommodations? I'll want to have a word with them before we send them off into the care of the magistrate."

Richards nodded and headed toward Sarah's assailant, while the coachman turned toward Hart's. Both "guests" would be bound and detained in an unused outbuilding, as far away from Sarah as Hart could keep them and under strict guard.

"Oh, ow," Sarah moaned, raising her head once again and releasing Hart. "My arm hurts."

Blood was trickling down her forearm toward her shoulder, soaking into the sleeve of her gown. He pulled his handkerchief from his pocket and pressed it to her wound. "Didn't even feel it when it happened, did you?"

She shook her head, then put a hand to the back of her head. "Is that normal? My head hurts, too, now."

"Completely. Your body was overwhelmed by shock and fear. Now that you're starting to calm down, you'll begin to notice aches and pains from your fight."

"You sound like you've experienced this yourself."

"I have." More times that he wanted her to know about.

"Are you experiencing it now?"

Hart did a mental check of his body parts. He might be a bit sore tomorrow from running—he couldn't remember the last time he'd run at his absolute top speed. But everything else seemed to be in working order. "No, not this time."

"Good," she said again.

"Can you walk? We should get that wound cleaned and bandaged, and I'll feel better when you're tucked safely into bed."

She nodded slowly, replacing his hand with her own to keep pressure on her arm. "I can walk. And

I think I'll feel better once I've been safely tucked into bed, too."

He slid his arm around her waist and drew her to him as they headed toward the house. Her shaking had lessened, but Hart knew it would be a long time before she was truly relaxed again.

"I tried to do what you taught me," she said, slipping her uninjured arm around his waist. "But I couldn't get my elbow in the right position, so I improvised."

He kissed her hair, catching a coppery whiff of blood from her attacker's nose. "And an excellent improvisation it was. I only wish you hadn't needed to do it."

"Me too. But it was a good thing you gave me that instruction."

A very good thing. As soon as he was done questioning their assailants, he was going to write up her next lesson in defense.

Hart sat in his study later that night swirling a glass of Irish whiskey, staring at the wall.

The two ruffians that had attacked them had little to say that Hart hadn't already heard from

Adam St. Peters—that proof of Sarah's death was to be taken to Seven Dials, London in exchange for one hundred pounds. They'd heard the story from some friends visiting from London shortly after the new Countess of Hartland arrived, and had done a little investigating. When they discovered that Lady Hartland was the former Sarah Shipton, they sprung into action.

A knock sounded on the closed door and Hart straightened in his chair. "Enter."

"You wanted to see me, my lord?" Richards halted just inside the door, his usual placid expression firmly in place.

"I did. Did our guests arrive at their destination?"

Richards had been tasked with overseeing the transfer of the attackers into the custody of the local magistrate. "They did, my lord. You'll need to be interviewed, as will Lady Hartland."

Hart nodded. He'd expected that, and hoped it could be done quickly. "Good. We're removing to Glanmire House. Lady Hartland and I will depart as soon as may be. You'll follow with her ladyship's maid and our baggage."

"As you wish, my lord."

"Be sure to pack the black brigandine that's out in my workshop. And all the small plates you can find." The brigandine needed repairing, and Hart had a special project in mind for the plates. He might as well work on both after they arrived in Ireland—there was no telling how long they'd be there.

"I will make sure they are included."

"Good man. And the air scrubbing mask, too. Perhaps I'll finally get that working."

"Certainly. Will there be anything else, my lord?"

Hart leaned back in his chair. "Not tonight."

"Then I will bid you a good night."

Richards turned toward the door and had it halfway open when Hart spoke again. "I almost lost her today, Richards. If those men had brought pistols instead of knives..."

"'Almost' being the operative word, my lord. Lady Hartland is safe and sound upstairs, and Mrs. Nichols assures me the wound on her arm will heal quickly and cleanly."

"You're right, of course. Good night, Richards."

The valet made his exit but Hart remained in his chair well into the night, swirling the liquid in his glass as he considered plans for their future.

Some were immediately discarded, like his overwhelming urge to ride hell-for-leather to London and track down the bastard that had issued the threat on Sarah's life. Some, like the equally overwhelming urge to never let Sarah out of his sight again, had a satisfying if twisted logic.

Whatever happened, he knew he had to be more prepared than he'd been tonight.

Chapter Ten

GLANMIRE HOUSE WAS located a few miles outside Cork, Ireland, several hundred miles and a body of water away from London and the person who wanted Sarah dead. The fact that Ireland often still felt like a separate country despite having been absorbed into the United Kingdom some twelve years before made Hart feel even better about his choice of retreat. Many of the locals wanted nothing to do with England or its people and would pay little heed to stories coming from its capital. He hoped that included murder for hire schemes.

Sarah seemed to be a country away from him at times, too. She practically—and sometimes literally—clung to him whenever he was in the main house, following him from room to room without ever seeming to settle in any of them. She also refused to leave the house for several days, even with an escort.

Hart supposed her behavior made sense. He remembered the first time he went up against a criminal as the Armored Man, how he felt as if he were being watched all the time, how every loud bang had reminded him of the pistol that had almost killed him. And he'd gone into that fight voluntarily. Sarah had been snatched from the arms of safety and thrust into danger without her consent.

But when they'd been in Ireland a little more than a week and Sarah was still acting as his shadow, he knew he had to do something to help her regain her balance. He missed the woman who demanded an explanation when he proposed marriage to her, who, when he became overprotective, promised not to put herself in harm's way without consulting him first.

And he suspected Sarah missed that version of herself, too.

Hart kept the promise he'd made to himself to teach Sarah more about defending herself, hoping that giving her more tools to use in dangerous situations might strengthen her confidence and sense of safety. He began escorting her to one of the grassy terraces behind the house where they worked on targeting weak spots on the body, how to use her smaller size to her advantage, and how much force she needed to use to make each action effective. She wore long-sleeved gowns each time despite the lingering summer warmth, hiding what she called the "disfigurement" on her arm. But each day her interest grew, and with it came renewed energy.

Then one day she came to him. Richards accompanied her, but she came of her own accord rather than having to be coaxed from the house. And he couldn't hold back his grin when she arrived in an old gown of faded green with short sleeves.

That's my girl.

When Richards had departed, Hart took Sarah's hands. "What shall we practice today, my love? Do you still think you can flip me over your shoulder?"

"Given enough leverage, I could flip you over the house," she smiled.

Hart's heart stuttered in his chest. How wonderful to see her smiling again! "I have no doubt you could. Do you want to give it a try?"

"I want to learn about weapons."

Hart felt his eyebrows shoot up to his hairline, but carefully reined them in. "Any weapon in particular?"

Sarah shook her head, but gave his hands a little squeeze. "I was hoping you would know what might work best for me."

He pretended to look her over as if he were appraising a new acquisition. "For you, I'd say a small pistol or a knife. I'm assuming you're looking for a defensive weapon rather than an offensive one."

"I have no desire to go after the people that hurt me, if that's what you're thinking. But I would like to be as prepared as possible in case someone else gets that close again."

Her voice was steady and her eyes were clear—she knew what she was asking. And he was happy to oblige her. "If Joanna Devlin hadn't gone abroad last week, I'd have her teach you to shoot. She's more competent with small arms than I am, and she could show you where to carry them on your person. But a dagger or stiletto... Come with me, and we'll see what we can find for you."

He drew her arm through his as if they were taking a leisurely stroll about the grounds and led her one more terrace up from the house, where his workshop and small forge were located.

"I have a nice selection of blades here," he indicated a large wooden chest pushed up against one wall of the workshop as they entered. "But if you don't find anything you like, I can make something to your specifications."

"A custom piece, just for me?"

She sounded delighted by the prospect, and Hart decided then and there to create the perfect blade for her. "Just for you. What would you like?"

"Let me see what my options are."

While Sarah rummaged through the chest, Hart busied himself making targets out of canvas leftover from the last brigandine he'd constructed there. She'd get a better feel for her weapon of choice if she could stab and slash at something other than the air.

"Something like this, I think," Sarah said, bringing over a small, stubby blade attached to a handle wrapped in wire. "It fits nicely in my hand and the wire makes for a firm grip. I just wish there was an easier way to carry it than in a scabbard like a tiny sword."

"There might be. Let me try a few things and see what I can come up with. In the meantime, let's work on your skills with that one."

"All right. What do I do? The only knives I've ever used were at the dinner table."

"Just like before, your objective is to make your assailant release you. Understand?"

She looked down at the weapon in her hand for a long moment, then raised her eyes to his and nodded. "Make him release me so I can 'run like hell.'"

"Exactly. With this type of blade you can thrust underhand or overhand, forward or backward." He placed himself behind her, slipping one arm around her waist as he showed her how to hold and thrust the knife in each instance.

The scent of flowery lemons clung to her as she set about following his instructions and Hart touched his nose to her hair, momentarily forgetting about the lesson.

"Hart?"

He kissed her crown and the tip of her ear. "May I ask you something?"

"Certainly."

She turned toward him and he should have released her, but couldn't bring himself to do so. "Are you well? I don't mean physically—I can see that your arm is fine. I mean, are you sleeping well at night? Do you find yourself reliving your attack? Are you interested in things other than learning to defend yourself?"

She set the knife on a table and slid her arms around him, meeting his gaze with her mouth pulled into a slight frown. "I am sometimes taken by a sudden flash in my mind of what happened, but that is happening less often now. And I've had Lucy sleeping in my chamber at night. Not that I think she'll afford me any protection, mind you, but it's calming to have another person there, to hear her breathing when I wake in the night."

"Why didn't you tell me?"

She laid a palm on his chest. "You have other things to worry about. I didn't want to add to your list."

"You are the list. Everything else can wait." Her brows rose in an unasked question and he tightened his arm around her, stroking her cheek with one hand. "Truly."

Her lips curved into a smile. "My mother said you would take excellent care of me. It seems she was right."

"You didn't believe her?"

"I possessed a healthy sense of skepticism. The only thing either of us knew about you was your reputation and your conduct in our shop." Sarah reached up to smooth his unruly hair. "I don't know if you've been hiding this side of you all these years or if it's newly developed, but I'm glad you've let me see it."

"What side of me?"

"The side that cares about people for who they are, not just what they can do for you."

He dropped his mouth to her ear and whispered, "I think that must be your influence, my lady."

"Sarah."

Hart straightened a little. "What?"

"You always call me 'my lady' when the conversation becomes intimate. Just once, I want to hear you say my name instead."

She was right. He had deflected and diffused emotions by using her title rather than her name. He kissed her cheek, her temple, and whispered, "You have done me a world of good, Sarah Jane Elliot. I'm not the same man you married, I'm becoming a better one."

She rested her cheek against his and held him close for what seemed like forever and mere seconds all at once. When she drew back she was smiling softly. "I'll take that knife with me back to the house and practice there for a while so you can focus and get some things done."

"You don't have to do that..."

"It's best, though, isn't it? Teaching me to defend myself isn't the only thing you need to do today, is it?

In addition to his promise to Sarah to keep her safe and find the coward who threatened her life, Hart did have estate business to tend to and a letter to send off to Wellington. His special project, too, was only partially complete.

Though he would have happily ignored it all to spend the afternoon with his wife. "I do have a few more things to tend to."

"Then I'll leave you to your work." She leaned up and kissed him softly—too briefly—on the lips. "Will you be joining me for dinner this evening?"

"I will."

"Then I'll see you in a few hours."

She pressed a kiss to his cheek, sheathing the blade of her knife as she made her way out of the workshop.

Hart turned to the target he'd made and grinned. "We'd better get to work, then."

Sarah ended up dining solo—again—but by this point in her marriage she'd become accustomed to eating her meals alone. She'd also come to realize that Hart's neglect of mealtime was simply that and not a reflection of his feelings for her. He hadn't said he loved her, but it was as clear to her as a bookshop ledger that he cared for her.

And she cared just as much for him.

He finally joined her in the drawing room after dinner, dressed in a charcoal gray coat, blue silk waistcoat, and white breeches. His top boots were polished to a high shine, his cravat and shirt snowy white. For Hart at home, this was fashion of the highest order.

"Who is this handsome gentleman in my drawing room?" she asked with a laugh.

He went down on one knee before her as she sat on the sofa. "'Tis I, your long lost husband, my lady, back from waging war on ledgers and decisions and a never-ending pile of correspondence."

She rose, reaching down to caress his cheek. "My Hartland? How do I know it's really you? Tell me something only he would know."

"You once tried to convince me to buy a copy of *Mad Man of the Mountain* because my library didn't have enough novels in it."

"It is you!" She raised him up like a queen with her subject then threw her arms around him in mock celebration, suppressing the very real laughter that bubbled up from her heart. She remembered well the day she offered him the novel, and the face he'd made upon reading its title. "I feared you'd been swallowed up by the heaps of paper in your study."

His arms came around her and his warm lips pressed against her temple. "I nearly was, but thoughts of you kept me strong."

Did she imagine the earnestness in his voice? "I'm so very glad you've returned to me," she replied softly.

"Did you miss me?"

"I always miss you when we're apart."

He pulled back to look her in the eyes. "You do?"

No more play-acting now. His tone was serious and she wanted to answer him. "Yes. I've always enjoyed your company—especially when I'm in your arms."

He flashed her a grin and kissed her, breaking away after a moment to mumble, "Is that so?" before capturing her lips again as if he'd truly been away for years rather than mere hours.

She pulled back to catch her breath and Hartland raised his eyebrows. "Is everything all right?"

In the whirlwind of danger and disgrace and few options, Sarah had let life happen to her since the day Hart compromised her. But here, now, she had the power to finally make a decision for herself. She summoned all the courage and brazenness she could find within her and told her husband what she wanted. "It will be when you take me to bed."

Hartland was silent for a long moment. Then he blinked. "Well, we did discuss my need for an heir."

He said it with a straight face, but Sarah laughed. "We discussed you *not* needing an heir. Have you changed your mind? Do you now wish to have one?"

"No. I wish to have you."

He leaned down and kissed her again, his passion and energy fueling the pounding of her heart. She tightened her arm about his neck, sliding her free hand through his dark hair as he broke away and feathered kisses across her cheek and down her neck.

"Say you want me, Sarah," he murmured against her ear.

She was no sheltered virgin and knew what he was asking, but her boldness faltered and she couldn't say the words aloud. Instead, she managed to breathe a "yes" when his hand cupped her breast through her gown.

"Yes what?"

She felt his mouth curve into a smile against her cheek and found herself grinning along with him. "Yes, I want you."

"Right here in the drawing room? Lady Hartland, you minx!"

She kissed his temple with a laugh, then pulled back just far enough to look him in the eyes. "Of course not. We should be upstairs, Hart."

He closed the short distance between them and kissed her again, grinning impishly when he drew away. "How perceptive of you, my darling—my bed is so much larger than the sofa, and we might very well need the space."

Scooping her up in his powerful arms, he stalked over to the door—pausing just long enough for Sarah to open it—and headed for the main staircase. Halfway up it he stopped and set her on her feet, sliding his arms around her waist and pulling her against his solid chest.

"I need another kiss."

"You can't wait the two minutes it will take us to reach your chamber?"

"No."

He went more slowly this time, as if he was savoring the sensation of her lips on his. One hand slid up her back to support her as he leaned into her, and she surprised herself by letting him take some of her weight. She felt secure in his arms, and gave herself up to the pleasure he was rousing in her.

They eventually made it to the master's suite and took turns removing articles of clothing from each other between kisses. When she was down to just her shift, Hartland, already naked, stood behind her and plucked the pins from her hair, combing his fingers through it when it tumbled down her back.

"If you want me to stop, you need to say it. I can't read your mind."

She smiled a little at that. "I suspect in this situation you could read my body with little trouble."

"Probably," he conceded, pushing her shift off her shoulders and down the length of her body, "but I want you to say it anyway."

"I will. But we can't stop what we haven't started."

That was all the encouragement he needed. Hartland picked her up and climbed onto the bed, laying her down in the center. He stretched out beside her, pushing the hair back from her face and kissing her again. Sarah reached out and wrapped him in her arms, moaning at the delicious friction when her breasts brushed against his chest as he pulled himself atop her. His body was warm and firm, the scent of mint and cloves lingering on his skin.

"There are so many things I want to do with you."

His voice was low and gruff. Sarah spread her legs a little wider and raised her knees, arching her back in an effort to get closer—if it was even possible—to Hart. She'd been this intimate with one other man in her life, but he'd never made her feel this...need.

"Pick one," she said with a grin, "and that's where we'll start."

"Start? I like the way you think."

"I'm your wife and you are my husband. We have the rest of our lives to work on your list."

He looked down at her, his dark eyes intent on her face. Had she said something wrong? Was he rethinking what they were about to do?

"Yes we do."

She felt his hardness at her entrance and he slowly eased himself in. He was a little thicker than she'd anticipated, but thankfully not so big as to be painful. When he was fully inside her he paused and she closed her eyes, soaking up the sensation of him.

"How do you feel?" he asked softly.

"So good," she smiled back. "Like I want to—like I *need* to move."

He nipped at her bottom lip. "Who am I to say no to my lady?"

She felt him slide out then slowly back in and she sucked in a breath. "Do that again." He obliged and she raised her knees a bit more, cradling his hips.

"More?"

"More."

He repeated the motion, then again and again. It felt... She couldn't come up with a suitable word for how it felt. She only knew she wanted to keep feeling it.

Hartland picked up speed, raising himself up a little more, increasing the space between their bodies. Sarah missed the feel of his hot skin against hers, but the sensation rising inside her distracted her from the loss. It was new and amazing, and felt as if it was building toward something even bigger.

She moaned and he grinned. "More?"

"Yes!"

And then something changed. The sensation in Sarah's body waned. Hart began to thrust a little faster, a little harder, and the pleasure she'd felt was chased away by pain.

"Hart, stop. You're hurting me."

He stilled immediately. "Oh, my love, I'm sorry. Are you all right?"

She nodded, her loose hair sliding against the pillow. "I will be in a minute, I think. You were just too...vigorous."

"More like too carried away with my own pleasure—how callous of me. But there's an easy way to fix that." He rolled them over so that Sarah was stretched out on top of him. "There. Now you're in charge."

"What?"

"Straddle me."

She smothered a giggle—no one had ever asked her to do that before—but complied, placing her knees on either side of Hart's hips and pushing herself off his chest. "Now what?"

"You decide. If you want to simply be still, then be still. When you're ready to move, use your legs to raise and lower yourself."

She tested his instruction, flexing her thighs to lift herself up and relaxing back against Hart's body. Better, but still a little painful. "I set the tempo."

"Yes."

"And the, erm, depth."

"Yes."

She did it again, but this time raising up only partway along his length before sliding back down. "That felt good."

"Yes."

He was grinning and she found herself smiling back. "Did you like that?"

"Oh yes."

He ran his hands down her bare back, the roughened pads of his fingers skimming her skin and sending shivers through her body. One hand came to rest on her hip and the other reached for her center. His thumb made contact with her most sensitive place and she gasped.

Hartland grinned again. "How did that feel?"

He touched her once more before she could answer. She reflexively threw back her head and arched her back. "Ohhh, Hart…"

He picked up a bit of moisture from their joining, continuing his ministrations until her breath came in shallow pants and a compulsion to move rose so powerfully in her she could not have defied it if she'd tried.

She went slowly at first, rising up only a couple of inches each time but increasing her speed as the pleasure built inside her. Bending forward to adjust the angle of her hips, she placed her hands on his chest and looked down into his dark eyes. He was strong and well-muscled beneath her, coiled and ready for more than what she was giving him. But there was no trace of domination on his face, no need to impose his will upon her.

Only desire.

Sarah dipped her head and captured his lips with hers, the rhythm of her hips faltering as she tried to coordinate the two movements. When her concentration shifted to her lower body, her mouth went slightly off course.

"Ow!" Hart pulled sharply back and pressed his fingertips to his bottom lip.

She froze. "What happened? Are you all right?"

"You bit me." He pulled his hand away and examined it. "No harm done, though. See?"

He showed her the absence of blood and she dropped a kiss on his fingers before carefully kissing the corner of his mouth. "I'm so sorry. We aren't doing this very well, are we?"

He laughed. "Just takes a little practice, my love. Shall we try it again?" He kissed her with a hunger that surprised her, running his hands through her long hair and over her backside.

She felt his heart pounding beneath her palms as his chest rose and fell in a pattern as ragged as her own breathing. Her lips curved into a self-satisfied smile. *She* had done that to him. "I think we'd better."

His hands continued to caress her as she resumed riding him, lifting herself higher and allowing him to stroke more deeply inside her. His hips matched her pace and they moved together, rebuilding that indescribable sensation within Sarah's body.

"That's it," Hart murmured, brushing her long hair from her face. "Let yourself go."

The sensation grew and she moved faster, urged on by her body as much as by Hartland. Her hands slid to his shoulders and held tight, as if she were afraid of being swept away.

And then she was.

The sensation peaked then broke over her in waves, stealing her thoughts, her control, her very breath, leaving her engulfed in the most magnificent pleasure. Hart thrust beneath her a few more times before she heard him gasp.

His arms came around her and drew her down to him. "My God, Sarah."

She relaxed against him, still intimately joined with him yet suddenly a little shy. "Is that good or bad?"

"It's good," he replied, kissing her hair. "Very, very good."

Hart woke during the night, unsure for a moment where he was or who he was with. His face was pressed into a pillow at the very edge of what he recognized as the big bed in his own chamber and a soft arm was curled around his waist. Rolling onto his back brought Sarah's sleeping face into view, and memories of their evening together warmed his groggy brain.

He picked up her hand from his abdomen and kissed it, rolling toward her and pulling her close. When she cuddled up against his chest and held him tightly, he remembered that they'd actually fallen asleep together several feet away in the middle of the bed. He'd always been a restless sleeper, particularly when a problem he wrestled with during his waking hours seemed impossible to solve. His previous bedfellows had rarely stayed long enough to be bothered by his thrashing, but the occasional lady that did stay had coped by moving to the far side of the bed, away from all the commotion.

Yet here was Sarah, as physically close to him as it was possible to be. He'd tossed and turned as usual, and she had simply hung on.

"You are a wonder, Sarah Elliott," he whispered. "And I am lucky to have you in my life."

Chapter Eleven

The woman slapped the newspaper down on the table in disgust. She'd bombed two other buildings in Town after the bookshop, careful not to let anyone see her planting the devices. People had died, the phosgene had been proven effective, yet no one affiliated with the Royal Army would see her or answer her letters regarding use of the gas. And now *The Times* was detailing Napoleon's invasion of Russia. Vilnius and Moscow had fallen without even a token resistance, and the French Emperor had begun his occupation of yet another country.

So much suffering. And none of it would have happened if David were alive.

Clearly grenades inside public buildings weren't enough. What to do instead? Give up on impressing the merits of phosgene upon the Army? Let Sarah Shipton—the woman would never think of her as the Countess of Hartland—enjoy her life as if nothing had ever happened?

Certainly not. Perhaps a different display of phosgene's power would be more persuasive.

Perhaps she hadn't been killing the right people to get noticed.

The woman picked up an earlier issue of *The Times* from the table and stared at the announcement of the marriage of the Earl of Hartland to Miss Sarah Shipton. Sarah had caused David's death and in return had wed a handsome aristocrat and become wealthier than she'd probably ever dreamed.

Well, there were ways to change that.

Sarah and her husband had fled London for Devon, so the woman's sources said. But the attempt there on Sarah's life had failed miserably, and she'd disappeared again. No one in the woman's network of criminals and spies had so far been able to locate Sarah or Hartland again.

"If I can't go to them, I'll just have to make them come to me." The woman smiled at the newspaper announcement. "Then Sarah Shipton will see what it's like to have her loved ones die in front of her."

Hart wandered into the chamber Sarah had taken as her private sitting room. Glanmire house was much larger than Hartland Abbey, and he'd been roaming the corridors for a handful of minutes trying to locate his wife. Or was he trying to locate his courage? And here she sat, curled up with a book as was her custom, a light breeze bringing in the sent of flowers from the gardens below.

"How is my beautiful bride this morning?"

"It's afternoon," she responded, arching a dark brow as she raised her eyes from her book.

No matter how intimate their relationship became, some things apparently never changed. "May I interrupt you for a moment?"

"You already have. But thank you for asking this time."

She was frowning instead of flashing him her usual smile, and Hart nearly abandoned his endeavor. He needed to tell her before she found out on her own, but if she was already unhappy about something her reaction to this would be even worse.

She placed a marker between the pages of her book and set it down on the chaise longue beside her. "What do you need?"

You. The answer came unbidden to his mind and he nearly said it aloud. But he needed to speak with her about something else, something less enjoyable than his feelings for her and the joy they brought each other in bed.

"I need to tell you something." He crossed the room and sat beside her on the chaise, taking one of her hands in his. He dearly wanted to kiss it, to wrap his arms around her and kiss her until they were both breathless, but he needed to make his confession and beg her forgiveness. "Your maid has been spying on you...at my behest."

"Yes, I know."

"What?"

Sarah reached for her book and removed a folded scrap of paper from between the pages, handing it to Hart. The handwriting was now all too familiar when he unfolded it. It was a note the maid had written describing her mistress's activities for the past few days.

"Lucy dropped this morning when she came to style my hair. When I questioned her about it, she told me you'd asked her to watch me and everyone around me. She said you asked her to report any suspicious activity or person directly to you, and to tell no one else what she was doing. I spent the whole afternoon trying to decide whether or not to confront you."

Sarah's face was set in a calm, cold expression that squeezed Hart's heart. "I can explain..."

"I wish you would."

Her voice wavered just a little, and Hart chastised himself yet again for being such an idiot. "I did ask your maid to watch you, and to watch who was near you, but not because I didn't trust you. You've been one of the more trustworthy people in my life, Sarah, even when you were just choosing my books."

"Then why did you force Lucy to spy on me? What did you hope to learn?"

"I'd hoped to learn who had threatened your life." He took her other hand and ran his thumbs over the backs of both of them. "I thought that perhaps someone would try to harm you by getting close to you. Mrs. Nichols chose the girl herself, after very careful consideration, so I knew she could be trusted. And a lady's maid is the closest person to her mistress, closer even than the lady's husband at times. She would know if someone was around who wasn't supposed to be, and I could take action. It was another way to keep you safe."

"That's what you were talking to her about the day we arrived at Hartland Abbey."

He'd spoken to the maid in Sarah's dressing room that day to confirm she would comply with his request. "You heard that?"

"Yes."

"I'm sorry."

"Because I heard you with Lucy or because you got caught invading my privacy and betraying my trust?"

"Everything," he replied without hesitation.

Her brows drew together and she took a deep breath, letting it out slowly the way she always did when she was trying to steady herself. "Why didn't you just tell me? Why go behind my back?"

He could see the pain on her face as clearly as he could feel it in his own chest. "I didn't want to worry you, Sarah. You had just found out that your mother lied to you and you were about to become penniless, and that someone wanted you dead. After marrying me and running away to Devon, I didn't know if you could handle the idea that someone in our own home could be a danger to you."

"Let's say I accept that explanation. We barely knew each other then, after all. Did you plan to tell me later?"

He pressed his lips together before answering. "No." It wasn't what she wanted to hear, but it was the truth. And he owed her that.

She withdrew her hands from his grasp. "It was my life in danger, my maid you had watching me. But you were never going to tell me?"

"It was for your own good, Sarah."

As soon as the words left his mouth he knew it was the wrong thing to say. She stood and put several feet of space between them.

"For my own good, you say? Am I a child? An imbecile? Am I so weak that you think to shelter me from my own life?"

Her voice rose in pitch and volume with each question, and Hart felt compelled to get to his feet. "You are none of those things. But I did think to spare you as much worry as I could, to keep unpleasant things from distressing you."

"The unpleasant things *in my own life!*" She stalked further away from him, positioning herself behind a chair as she clutched its back. "Have you kept other things from me?"

"Yes."

"Things that affect me?"

"Yes."

"You have as little respect for me as my mother did. But you managed to tell her the truth when you sent her north."

It was getting harder and harder to look her in the eye, and she did him the favor of turning away. He ran his hands through his hair and dropped back onto the chaise. Idiot was too mild—he'd easily regressed to heartless bastard.

"Tell me."

She'd turned to face him again, her hands clutching the back of the chair and her chin raised, looking for all the world like Wellington must have after his troops rampaged through Badajoz.

Hart hesitated another moment, then decided to obey. If she wanted to know everything he would tell her *everything*. Perhaps then she'd understand why he'd kept it all from her in the first place.

"All right. Where should I start?"

"The letters you received at Hartland Abbey, the ones that drove you into your workshop day and night."

The first of many, as it had turned out. "One was from Ollie, informing me that a shop in Bond Street had been bombed. The bombs had released some kind of gas and no one knew what it was. The second was from a contact of mine you haven't met providing more details. Four people died as a result of the gas in the shop—their lungs filled with fluid until they could no longer breathe."

Her face paled, but she held fast to the chair. "And that is why you wanted to make a mask that could clean the air. To save people if it happened again."

"Yes."

"And the other letters you received by 'special messenger'?"

"Those were updates from other contacts. There were two other bombings after the first. The second one killed four more people, and the third killed eight."

She moved around the chair and sat herself down. "How awful."

"And I can't get my mask to work."

"How awful," she said again, more softly this time. Hart thought perhaps he heard a note of sympathy as well, but that could have been wishful thinking.

And there was more. "Three days ago, a man was caught trying to dispose of Lady Ashfield's body, and that of her coachman. When questioned by the magistrate, this man admitted to abducting her from her carriage during her drive to Hartland Abbey and killing her along with her coachman. He thought she was you."

Whatever color was left drained from Sarah's face.

But Hart wasn't done. "He'd removed her head and intended to transport it to Seven Dials to collect his reward."

"Oh God," she whispered.

"Then today," he continued, gaining momentum, "I received another letter from my contacts in London. One person has claimed responsibility for all three bombings. Sarah, it was Lady Rebecca Barrington."

She didn't reply, didn't seem to react at all. Then she seized the arm of her chair and leaned heavily against it. "Lady Rebecca? She's an earl's daughter. Diana said she was very popular among the *ton* and does a lot of charity work. Why would she bomb shops in London?"

"I don't know. But she's also threatened Diana."

Sarah's head jerked up. "What?"

How was he going to tell her that her best friend's life was now in just as much danger as her own? "A letter was posted anonymously to the

Talbot household demanding your return to London in exchange for Diana's life."

"And you think it was Rebecca?"

"Diana recognized the handwriting."

Sarah's mouth pulled into a frown. "Someone could have forged it. How did Lady Rebecca claim responsibility for the bombings?"

"She sent a letter to several newspapers, and they all printed it."

"Then how do you know it was really her? Anyone could have sent those letters."

He knew she was going to ask that. And he was prepared to answer her question. "A friend of mine is verifying it as we speak."

Sarah dropped her head into her hands, and Hart waited for the sound of her sobbing to fill the room. He stood and started toward her when she took a deep breath and raised her eyes to his.

"If someone in London knows all of this, then I assume Lady Rebecca has been arrested."

Hart shook his head. "She's disappeared. None of my contacts have been able find her so far."

"Is she the one who sent those men after me?"

"That hasn't been confirmed yet, but it makes sense. Diana's letter arrived after the attack on us in Hartland failed and you remained alive."

Sarah's shoulders slumped. "I don't understand... She tried to help us when we were caught together at Lord Preston's ball."

"I know this must be difficult..."

Hart didn't get to finish his thought. Sarah was on her feet in the blink of an eye, coming to a halt just inches away from him. "You said you only found out today about the threat to Diana. Were you going to tell me about that?"

"I-I hadn't decided."

"My closest friend in the world was told she'd die if I didn't travel to London, and you—" She poked him in the chest hard with her index finger. "—weren't sure if you wanted to tell me? You really do think me weak."

"Not you, me," he replied softly, realizing the truth as he spoke the words. "I was barely holding myself together. Each new letter sent me reeling again, and it was all I could do not to bury myself in my workshop and never come out."

She folded her arms across her chest and pressed her lips together as if she didn't believe him.

Hart reached for her, sliding his hands down her shoulders. "You were the only thing keeping me from insanity, Sarah. And I didn't have the strength to tell you, to burden you with all of this."

"You're telling me now."

"My conscience finally became louder than my cowardice."

She was unyielding beneath his hands. "Do I know everything now?"

Everything except his part in Wellington's intelligence gathering ring. He'd been sworn to secrecy on that but part of him wanted to tell her anyway, to lay it all out for her. "Everything that directly relates to you, yes."

"That sounds like a dodge. What aren't you telling me, Hartland?"

"I belong to a clandestine organization that gathers information to keep the realm safe and help win the war." He dropped his hands from her shoulders. "I can't tell you any more—I shouldn't even tell you that much. But now you know everything."

She was silent, her face set in a neutral expression. He'd expected tears by now, or at least some nervous pacing, but she wasn't showing any indication of either.

"All right, then. What is our plan? How are we going to deal with Lady Rebecca?"

"Not 'we', Sarah. Me, with some help from my contacts and Ollie."

"But I must stay away, where I'm safe and won't bother you?" She stalked away from him, almost stomping around the room for a few moments before returning to her original place before him. "Remember when we had our first picnic near your workshop in Hartland? I told you then that I was stronger than I looked."

And not just physically, it seemed.

She squared her shoulders and continued, "If it were you and Major Oliver under threat, you'd handle the problem yourself, wouldn't you?"

"Of course I would," he replied. Where was she going with this line of thought?

"Then allow me to participate in my own defense and to defend my friend." He opened his mouth to protest, but she held up a finger to quiet him. "I know I don't have your fighting skills or training with weapons. But there are other things I can do."

She made an excellent point there. Her knowledge of chemistry far surpassed his own, and she was infinitely better with people than he was. In dealing with a woman who liked to bomb populated targets with some strange gas, both those attributes could become assets. And if he were in her place, he'd certainly rail against being excluded. Perhaps she could be a part of stopping Lady Rebecca without putting herself in danger. After betraying Sarah's trust the way he had—the way her mother had at the start of all of this—he owed her some sort of inclusion.

"Yes, there are other things you can do, and I will happily avail myself of those things." He took both her hands in his and gave them a gentle squeeze. "Just remember that I promised to keep you safe, and I intend to keep that promise."

She didn't kiss him or embrace him or even smile at him, she simply nodded and withdrew her hands. "I know."

Neither of them spoke for several more moments, and the silence became awkward between them.

"I'll let you get back to your book," he told her, gesturing to where it lay on the chaise. "Will you meet me in my study after dinner this evening? We can go over what we know about the situation and begin to form our plan."

"I'll be there."

"Good. Until this evening, then." He bowed clumsily and showed himself out of the chamber.

Did she hate him? Was she indifferent to him? After what they'd shared together, and not just in the bedchamber, both possibilities hurt. All the more so because he had brought them on himself. It didn't matter that he'd tried to tell Sarah about his deal with her maid before today, or that he really did have her safety in mind. She was right—he'd treated her like a weak child. Just like her mother had done.

Well, he'd live with the consequences. As long as Sarah was safe and unharmed, nothing else mattered. And when her situation was dealt with once and for all, Hart would spend the rest of his life trying to make it up to her.

Chapter Twelve

"My lady, you're needed in the library."

Lucy's voice was tentative, as if she expected to be relieved of her position at any moment. It didn't seem to matter that Sarah didn't hold any ill will toward the girl—she'd only been following her employer's orders, after all. But then, it had only been a few hours since her pact with Hartland had been revealed.

Sarah suppressed a sigh and tried to keep her voice calm. She was furious with Hartland, but she didn't want to take it out on Lucy. "Do you know why?"

"Something about books, my lady. They arrived for his lordship, but he said you should take care of them."

Of course he did. Hartland had immediately retreated to his workshop after their conversation. He'd likely ordered something earlier in the month and no longer wanted to remain in the house long enough to deal with it.

"Thank you, Lucy. I'll go down in a few moments."

The maid darted out of the room and Sarah dropped her head into her hands. She'd only just resumed her seat on the chaise longue in her sitting room after hiking the length and breadth of Glanmire House's large park—with a sturdy footman as her bodyguard—trying to burn away her anger. She'd succeeded only in tiring herself out. Her anger toward Hartland, and toward her mother if she was completely honest, blazed even hotter and had taken on a measure of emotional pain. They were two of the three people in her life that she trusted the most, and they'd both stomped all over that trust. They'd taken away what little control she had over her own life and hoarded it for themselves.

The two people she loved most in the world didn't give a damn about what she wanted.

The tears came then, hot and fast, and with such force Sarah couldn't stop them. A month's worth of pent up fear and rage and grief, all the emotions she had pushed down to deal with at a more convenient time, poured out of her in a torrent. She covered her face, pressing a hand against her mouth as her shoulders shook, trying to muffle the sobs wrenched from her throat.

She didn't know how long she sat there, but her eyes and lungs ached when the tears finally dried up. The anger she'd tried so hard to dispel with her hike had died to embers, perhaps out of sheer exhaustion. Those embers still burned, but they were now accompanied by a sense of composure. Hartland might control her life, but only she held dominion over her person.

And her person wanted to investigate the library. She headed to her bedchamber to wash her face and stretch her stiff body. If there really were new books, she didn't just want to leave them lying around in whatever disarray Hartland had no doubt left them. And it would give her something to think about besides the fact that both her mother and husband had kept life-altering information from her.

For her own good.

When she arrived in the library, she was greeted by the housekeeper, Mrs. McKenney, who stood among an array of large wooden boxes. Some had their lids already off, revealing stack upon stack of leather-bound books.

"What is all this?" Sarah asked. When Lucy had said there were books in the library, Sarah had envisioned a few or even as many as a dozen. But there were at least ten boxes scattered across the floor and tables, each containing what looked to be twenty books.

"I was hoping you'd know, my lady," Mrs. McKenney replied. If she noticed Sarah's red eyes, she was astute enough not to mention them. "The men who delivered all this said it was for his lordship from Hartland Abbey, but his lordship said it was all for you. What do you suppose it means?"

Sarah pushed back a lid that had already been pried off and rummaged through the contents. "This one is all novels..." She moved to another box and repeated the process. "...and these are mathematics texts."

The housekeeper joined in, opening the box nearest her. "These are all in another language, my lady."

Sarah leaned over for a look. "French, I'd say. Does Hartland even read French?"

Mrs. McKenney shrugged and started to reply, but cut herself off. "Oh look, here's a letter."

Sarah accepted the folded paper and opened it. The note was brief and addressed to Hartland, but she recognized the handwriting. It belonged to Mr. Higgins.

"These are books from my parent's bookshop," she said softly, never taking her eyes from the letter. "It looks to be what was left of our inventory."

"His lordship sent you a bookshop?"

Mr. Higgins's note was dated several weeks prior. Hartland must have made arrangements to purchase the books and have them transported to the Abbey before or shortly after they'd left London, then had them sent on to Glanmire House. Thoughtful of him, particularly since he hardly knew her at that point.

Though it seemed he still didn't know her that well. "It appears so."

"Then you'll be needing help putting these all away." Mrs. McKenney gathered her skirts in one hand and picked her way among the boxes toward the door. "I'll send a couple of footmen to help you, my lady."

"Oh no, that won't be necessary." Shelving her parents' books would soothe her aching heart. It would almost be like walking among the shelves in their shop again. "Perhaps you could send them in later to help with the boxes, though."

"As you wish."

Mrs. McKenney departed and Sarah was left alone with the books she'd been surrounded by every day of her life before her marriage to Hartland. The fragrance of the wooden boxes mingled with the smell of leather covers and the pages they held. As she moved about the room extracting books from their boxes and finding homes for them on Hartland's bookcases, the scent and the feel of the books in her hand calmed her further.

By the time she'd emptied half of the boxes, Sarah felt like she was in full control of herself again. Hartland was still her best option for dealing with the people hunting her and the one—could it really be Lady Rebecca?—who wanted her dead. He had the contacts, the training, and the experience to keep her physically safe and track the woman down to put an end to the havoc she was wreaking. Once Rebecca was contained and her order for Sarah's death nullified, Sarah could go anywhere, do whatever she pleased. Hartland had promised her separate lives, after all.

But Sarah would no longer be a passive bystander in her own life. If she could take control in the bedchamber, she could take control outside it, too.

She was waiting for him when he entered his study, already seated at the big mahogany desk that dominated the room.

"And here I thought I was early for a change," he said lightly.

"You are, actually." Her voice sounded nearly as tense as her body felt. The equanimity she'd experienced after she'd cried out her anger and frustration had vanished the moment her husband walked in the door.

He stood before her, several feet from the desk with his hands clasped behind his back. "Shall we get started?"

Her determination to take control of her own life was still firmly in place. "Yes. We should start with the bombs. If we can find a way to neutralize the gas Lady Rebecca is putting inside them, that will minimize casualties the next time she uses them."

Hartland pulled a chair over and parked it beside the desk, dropping into it with a nod. "That gives us time to find her. Good idea."

"It may also tell us something about where she is."

He reached around to the front of the desk, unlocking the end drawer with a small key and removing a sheaf of papers. "One of the letters I received gave the name of the gas. Apparently Lady Rebecca was keen to extol its virtues as a weapon and wrote some sort of manifesto to the Royal Army. Ah, here it is. She called it 'phosgene'."

"Phosgene?" Thank the heavens! This would be an easy problem to solve. "That was the subject of John Davy's paper—the one that his brother gave to the Royal Society earlier this year. Mr. Davy produced a gas when he exposed a mixture of carbonic oxide and chlorine to light, and he called it phosgene."

"Oh yes, I remember now."

"He said it caused his eyes to water a lot and become painful."

Hartland leaned back in his chair, gazing steadily at Sarah. "And if the gas caused his eyes to water and sting, imagine what it could do to the lungs."

"I'd wager a month's pin money that Lady Rebecca thought the same thing."

"Well, she was right. Did Davy say how to decompose it?"

Sarah reached for the stack of chemistry texts she'd brought with her from Glanmire's library and ran a finger down the books' spines. "Here it is.

Let's have a look and see." Skimming through the words, she found not one but two ideas that might be of use. "According to Mr. Davy, both ammonia gas and water will decompose phosgene. Combining it with the ammonia produces a neutral salt—"

"That would be easy to deal with."

"—and a lot of heat."

"That could be a problem."

He was trying to be funny, to break the tension that had grown between them, but Sarah didn't give him the laugh or smile he was looking for. "If the ammonia didn't kill people first. But decomposing phosgene in water produces carbonic oxide and muriatic acid." Carbonic oxide gas wasn't something one wanted to breathe in, but it wouldn't burn one's lungs like phosgene had reportedly done.

Hartland stretched his legs out in front of him and crossed them at the ankle. "Carbonic oxide can be dispersed easily as long as it's outside or in a building with windows that open. What about muriatic acid?"

"It's a liquid at the temperature of this room. We should be able to neutralize it with a base, as one would when one has a case of indigestion."

"Which base?"

That was a question Sarah couldn't answer. If anyone had done any sort of experimentation with this particular substance, she didn't know about it. "Locate some muriatic acid, and I'll find out."

"Know your way around a laboratory, do you?"

She didn't think he meant his comment to sound condescending, but it did. And she was not in the mood to be gentle with him. "Know your way around acids and bases, do you?"

He smiled, but it was more subdued than usual. "Fair point. What shall we do, then?"

"If you will set up a laboratory space where I can test out different bases and be safe, I will perform the experiments myself."

His smile became a frown. He was probably picturing her being ravaged by some horrible chemical spill, as if she wasn't intelligent enough to think of wearing protective clothing.

"Will part of my workshop do?"

"That will be fine."

"Would you like to begin your work tonight?"

He almost certainly wouldn't be able to procure the muriatic acid so quickly, and Sarah was tempted to take him up on his offer simply to see the look on his face. But there was other work to be done before she could begin experimenting. "Tomorrow will be soon enough. I'll need to find out what bases are commonly found around the estate first, anyway. A substance does us no good if it's hard to find."

Hartland rose from his chair. "I'll see to it."

Her body relaxed when he'd shut the door behind him, leaving her alone in the study. She was glad that they could still hold a civil conversation with one another, but the effort of doing so was draining.

Did she have the strength to keep this up?

Hart moved about his workshop without paying much attention to his actions, clearing an assortment of tools and materials from a table while his mind dwelled firmly upon his wife.

Sarah had been polite and interested in the discussion, but there had been none of the smiles or casual touches that he'd come to enjoy. When he'd reached for the desk drawer she'd actually stiffened, as if she didn't want him any nearer to her than absolutely necessary. Was she now repulsed by him?

"I wish Ollie were here."

Talking a situation over with Ollie always helped, whether the issue was criminals or women or which entertainment to attend. What would Ollie tell Hart to do in this instance?

"He'd tell me to apologize to Sarah," Hart said to the broken gauntlet he held. "I already told her I was sorry, but Ollie would say that wasn't enough. He'd say that words are easy for a glib blackguard like me, and if I really was remorseful I'd find a way to prove it to her."

Hart stopped beside the table he was clearing and leaned against it, running his hand over the battered surface. The books from her mother's shop were a good start, but he'd arranged for their purchase and transportation before he started hiding important information from Sarah. The same went for the project he'd been working on for her. He needed to do something now, after he'd transgressed and confessed.

"I could increase her pin money." He dropped a box of odds and ends and shoved it across the floor. "That's too easy, though. And it wouldn't mean anything to her. She's barely spent a shilling since we were wed, despite my offer to have a dressmaker, or anyone else, wait upon her at Hartland Abbey."

He found a wooden chair in the corner of the workshop and dragged it to Sarah's table. "What, then, would be difficult for me? What would involve my pain? My humiliation?"

Hart shook his head. "Ollie would tell me to stop thinking this was about me. It's about Sarah."

And what did Sarah want? What would mean the most to her?

What had Hart so carelessly taken from her?

The minute he compromised her at Preston's ball, Hart had taken control of nearly every aspect of Sarah's existence.

"She could have said no when I proposed marriage."

But could she really? She'd have been a pariah, no longer respectable enough to even work in her mother's shop, if the shop hadn't been closing. And that was another thing she'd had no control over—her mother had let Sarah's financial security slide away and actively covered it up, determined that Sarah should never know what had happened.

"Oooohhhh..."

Yes, that would be perfect. It would give Sarah the control over her own life she'd been denied and cause Hart a great deal of anxiety. That it was difficult for him to do—and that she would know *how* difficult—would make it even more significant.

Now, where was she?

Hart trotted back to the main house and burst in through kitchen door. The place was alive with activity as servants rushed around preparing a meal. Which meal? What time was it?

"Has anyone seen Lady Hartland?" he asked the room at large.

All motion and sound ceased, and every eye turned to Hart.

"I just sent a tray up for her, my lord," the cook replied. "She should be in her bedchamber."

Her bedchamber? He glanced out the window and noticed how much brighter the sky had become since he'd gone out to his workshop. Breakfast, then.

"Thank you."

He left the kitchen and headed for Sarah's suite, with a quick stop at his own chamber to retrieve the special project he'd created for her. When he arrived at her door, he forced himself to pause for the count of five before knocking.

"Sarah, it's Hart."

There was nothing but silence for what seemed like an eternity, then she opened the door herself. "What do you want?"

She was fully dressed—still keeping merchants' hours, apparently—in a pretty pink gown with little flowers sewn into the material, though the expression on her face was less cheerful.

"May I come in?"

She held the door wide for him and gestured with her free hand, eyeing the wrapped package he carried without speaking.

He set the package down on her bed and clasped his hands together behind his back. "I owe you an apology."

"You owe me nothing," she responded evenly. "I am your wife, and you may treat me however you wish."

"My wish is to make you happy and keep you safe. And I haven't been particularly successful in either endeavor."

Was it his imagination or did her face soften slightly? "You have kept me safe, Hartland, even through the attack. If it weren't for you, I'd undoubtedly be dead by now."

"Safe, then, but not happy." When she didn't reply he picked the parcel up off her bed and handed it to her. "I know that nothing I say or do will excuse the way I treated you—excuses are for poltroons with no spines."

She accepted the parcel, but held his gaze. "And you're not one of those."

"No. Not anymore. Go ahead and open it."

She tore the wrapping away with little enthusiasm. "Stays?"

"Not just any stays," he told her, stepping closer and turning out part of the garment's interior. "Armored stays."

The entire inside of the corset was covered with small pockets, each one holding a small plate of steel like those he used for his brigandines. He'd reduced the size and added some curve to the plates where he was able so the garment would lay flat against Sarah's body.

"If any of the plates need adjusting, if they don't feel right when you wear it, I can fix them."

"You made this for me?"

"I had a seamstress in Hartland copy one of yours," he confessed with a sheepish smile. "And your maid sewed the pockets."

"But you armored a corset for me."

Was she pleased? He couldn't tell. "I did. It won't be as easy to wear as a brigandine—though

I'll make you one of those, too, if you want one. But you can wear it anywhere and no one will ever know it's there."

Her eyes widened and she loosened the laces, running her fingers along the rows of stitches holding the pockets in place. "This isn't something I can get into quickly. I'd need to know in advance when I was going to be in danger."

"That's the downside…and why I'll also make you the brigandine. But I thought it might come in handy—"

"—if we went off the property again."

"Yes."

She examined every inch of the corset from the inside out, then held it up against her body. It was all he could do to from picturing her in it…and nothing else.

"Thank you." Sarah lifted her eyes to his. "I'll have Lucy help me put it on and make sure it fits properly."

He longed to make a joke about helping her take it off, but even he knew that now was not the time. Instead, he offered up his own soul. "It comes with an apology, if you'd like to hear it."

She crossed to the bed, almost within his reach, and laid the stays down. "I would."

"Husband or not, no one should be keeping secrets of such a great magnitude from you. A surprise gift," he gestured to the corset, "is one thing, but to withhold information about your very life is beyond contemptible. No one would even consider doing such a thing to me, so it wasn't until you called me out for my behavior that I realized how awful it was."

"Called you out?" she asked with a small smile. "Are we to fight a duel?"

"No." He took a step forward. "A duel is fought when the offending party will not apologize for his offense, when he will not take steps to make right his wrong. I am so very sorry for keeping things from you, Sarah, and for the pain that I've caused you."

He took her hands, stroking her skin with his thumbs. "You are the brightest part of my life, and I want to be the brightest part of yours. Can you forgive me for my stupidity?"

Her blue eyes swept over his face and she squeezed his hands. "I do believe you mean that."

"Every word."

She was quiet for a long moment before replying. "I am angry, Hartland, and I cannot simply let my anger go because you are repentant.

Nor can I reinstate my trust in you as if nothing had happened."

"Then I will earn back your trust." He'd make it his highest priority, after her safety.

"I hope so," she said softly.

"Let's start with this: we need a plan to apprehend Lady Rebecca. Would you like to put it together?"

"Me?"

"You know her better than I do, and you are the one she's been hunting. It's only fitting that you be the one to orchestrate her arrest."

Sarah withdrew her hands and moved to her dressing table, picking up her hairbrush and toying with the bristles. "Would I be working alone?"

"If you'd like to. All of the information my contacts have gathered would be at your disposal."

She faced him, leaning back against the table. "You'd allow me to work out the whole thing without you?"

It would pain him more than he would admit to not be the one planning Lady Rebecca's capture, to let someone else take the lead. But that would be less painful than living with Sarah's disdain. "If that's what you want."

"What if I need your help?"

There was a note of suspicion in her voice and he immediately tried to allay it. "All you'd have to do is ask."

"And there would be no judgment on your part? No insinuation that I was weak because I couldn't do it alone?"

"No more than when Ollie needed help walking after he was wounded." He slung his arm around the post at the foot of her bed. "I will assist you as I assisted him."

There was no greater vow he could make to her than that, and Hart was pleased when she acknowledged that fact with a single nod.

"Then I will get started today."

Chapter Thirteen

"LADY HARTLAND, HIS lordship has requested your presence in his study."

Sarah looked up from the notebook she was writing in to see Richards standing just inside the door of Hartland's workshop, several yards from the table she'd been working at.

"When am I to present myself?"

"As soon as may be, my lady. He says there is news about a certain situation you are interested in, and someone he'd like you to meet."

Richards punctuated his speech with a meaningful look, and Sarah realized he meant *her* situation. Who was she to meet? What news did this person bring?

"I'll be there directly."

Richards disappeared and Sarah carefully tidied the area where she'd been conducting her experiments. Her thoughts spun round and round as she hurried across the manicured grass and through the large house. Had Rebecca been caught? Had she bombed another shop? Had the letters to the newspapers been a hoax perpetrated against her?

Hartland opened the door to the study himself when Sarah knocked, resting his hand against the small of her back as he drew her into the room. "This is the Joanna I wanted you to meet," he murmured, placing a kiss on her temple. "Don't say anything about that in front of our other guest, though. I'll explain it all later."

She gave him a small nod, then put on a shy smile for the benefit of the man and woman awaiting them in the middle of the room. "I beg your indulgence for a newly wed couple. Perhaps Hartland will one day be able to introduce me to people without such displays of affection, but not today."

The man shifted from one foot to the other, looking noticeably uncomfortable. But the woman was wearing a sly smile in addition to her expensive looking black gown.

"You have it," she replied. "It's nice to see Hartland so happy."

Sarah was about to reply, but her husband gave her a little squeeze and ushered her toward the two strangers. "Lady Hartland, may I present to you Mrs. Perkins and Mr. MacDonald."

Mrs. Perkins curtsied. "Call me Joanna, please. Hartland does often enough."

"Of course," Sarah said automatically. What kind of relationship did her husband have with this woman? And how was she involved in Sarah's predicament? "I hope you'll call me Sarah. There's no need to stand on ceremony with an old friend."

Mr. MacDonald offered Sarah a nod, and took her hand when she offered it. "It's a pleasure to meet you, my lady. If you don't mind I will stand on ceremony a bit, since I am a stranger to you all."

Hartland led the small party to a pair of sofas upholstered in heavy green velvet, set at right angles to each other. "I think this conversation will be easiest if we're all seated comfortably."

"What conversation?" Sarah asked.

"Lady Rebecca Barrington," Mr. MacDonald answered, "and her phosgene gas."

He said the word slowly, in two distinct syllables, as if it was unfamiliar in his mouth: phos-gene. He probably didn't have much, if any, scientific training. What could he contribute?

"Start from the beginning," Hartland told him.

"My brother David was betrothed to Rebecca," Mr. MacDonald began. "She worked with him in his laboratory trying to find a way to put an end to this bloody war with the French, and end the war with the Americans before it grew further. David would explain to me the ideas they had, but I didn't understand much of it. Then, a few months ago, he became very excited about a new gas he'd read about called phosgene. It wasn't his ideal way to end a war, but after testing it in various situations he was convinced that phosgene was so dangerous the French and the Americans would surrender rather than subject their soldiers and sailors to it."

Sarah glanced at Hartland sitting beside her. Here was corroboration of two pieces of his information, but he was frowning at Mr. MacDonald. "Then what happened?"

"He took a trip to Dover to visit our grandmother, and brought some of his experiments with him to continue working on them. I never did get all the details from Rebecca—she'd gone with him—but it seems he was pushed by a woman in the street and the vials of phosgene he was carrying broke open. No one else was injured, but David breathed in the gas that was released and succumbed a few days later."

Sarah's whole body went rigid. Pushed in the street in Dover? Broken vials? It couldn't be...

"Sarah?"

Hartland's hand was warm as it clasped hers, and though she was still angry with him for his deception, she was glad for that show of support. He could easily have held this meeting without her, but he chose to include her so she could hear Mr. MacDonald's story firsthand. He could also have sent her away at the first sign of distress, but instead he attempted to comfort her.

She squeezed his hand in hers. "I think I was the one David MacDonald met in Dover. Remember? I bumped into a well dressed gentleman carrying a box, and heard glass break when he dropped it."

"You didn't push him?" Mr. MacDonald asked, his eyes wide.

Sarah turned toward him and shook her head. "I wasn't watching where I was going, and the collision was entirely my fault. But when I offered to replace anything that had been broken, the gentleman insisted there was no harm done."

"That sounds like my brother. Can you describe him?"

It had been a short encounter, but Sarah did her best to recall features beyond his height and hair color. "The lid of the box had 'Garwell & Sons' stenciled on it."

"That's the name of our grandfather's shipping business," Mr. MacDonald confirmed quietly.

This was the verification they needed. A single chance meeting in Dover had set everything in motion, including the death of Mr. MacDonald's brother. She managed to murmur, "I'm so sorry," but a lump grew in her throat that prevented her from speaking further. It had been an accident, certainly, but Sarah was responsible for the death of a man. If she had simply watched where she was going, David MacDonald would be alive today.

"Is that really what killed him, then?" Mr. MacDonald asked. "This phosgene that Rebecca talked about?"

Sarah swallowed hard, forcing the lump down. "It's possible. If the box wasn't airtight some of the gas could have escaped, even if he didn't open it. If he inhaled enough, it certainly could have been lethal. In fact, he may have saved my life by brushing me off and keeping me away from the box."

Mr. MacDonald smiled. "That sounds like him. He always wanted to make the world better, safer for people. If he knew what he was carrying was dangerous, he'd have insisted no one handle it but him."

"Didn't you say your brother was betrothed to Lady Rebecca?" Joanna asked. When Mr.

MacDonald nodded, she turned to Sarah. "If she believes you were responsible for the death of her fiancé it would explain why she wants you dead—a woman in pain would want retribution for her loss."

But Sarah couldn't quite reconcile the Lady Rebecca that had spoken for her at Diana's ball with the woman who considered her a killer, and had killed so many people herself.

"If what Mr. MacDonald says is true." Sarah turned her gaze on him. "I mean no offense, but you have every reason to suspect that Lady Rebecca had a hand in your brother's death. You could easily be feeding us a Banbury tale to avenge him."

"I could," Mr. MacDonald responded, "but I'm not. I admit that I do not like Rebecca, and that I didn't want David to marry her. But she loved him more than anything else in the world, and she would never hurt him. I'm sure of that."

His voice was even and his eyes met Sarah's as he spoke. Either he was a practiced liar or he was telling the truth.

"Joanna?" Hartland asked.

"Lady Rebecca had no family, but Miss Talbot is a close friend. She verified Rebecca's feelings for

David MacDonald and the trip to Dover. She said the betrothal was a secret, so Rebecca could not have mourned publicly. Rebecca was distraught after David's death, but because of the secret, was determined not to show it."

Mr. MacDonald nodded slowly. "David was worried our grandfather would think he was marrying an earl's daughter for the prestige she would bring, and that he was ashamed of our family because we are in trade. They each promised to tell only one person until David could win over Grandfather. David chose me. Rebecca must have chosen Miss Talbot."

"Hartland?" Sarah asked, squeezing his hand.

"I'm convinced. That's why Joanna brought him out here instead of writing it all in a letter, isn't it?"

Joanna nodded. "It would have been dangerous to have this information in writing. But yes, I did also think you should hear it directly from Mr. MacDonald."

"What happens now?" Mr. MacDonald asked.

"You will be my guest for as long as you like," Hartland answered. "And we are going to find Rebecca."

His use of the word "find" triggered something in Sarah's mind. "What if we don't have to find her. What if we can make her come to us?"

Joanna sat up a little straighter. "What are you thinking?"

"Something showy. Something that will have the whole of London talking. Hartland, when was the last time you hosted a ball?"

Joanna laughed and Hartland pressed his lips together the way he did when he was thinking hard. "I'd have to say...never. Why?"

Sarah grinned. "Then I think it's time you did."

Hart stared at his wife. She wanted to throw a party to catch a criminal? One who had killed numerous people already, and also wanted her dead. That didn't make any sense. Why put a large population at risk when they didn't have to?

Fortunately, Joanna voiced his thoughts in a much less condescending way than he would have. "How would it work?"

"What does Rebecca want more than anything else in the world?"

Joanna's face lit with understanding. "She wants you dead. But no one has killed you yet, so perhaps she'd come and do it herself."

Hart saw Sarah flinch ever so slightly at Joanna's blunt phrasing. It couldn't have been easy talking about one's own person as a potential murder victim. But the idea was a good one. If Lord and Lady Hartland held a big, attention-grabbing event, Rebecca would have a hard time resisting the opportunity to go after Sarah.

"We could say we were celebrating our marriage," Sarah continued, turning her blue eyes on Hart. "The fact that I'm alive to dance with my adoring husband while she can't even wear black for her deceased fiancé ought to bring her out in the open. "

"That makes you the lure," Hart said more sharply than he'd meant to.

Sarah was still holding his hand and gave it a squeeze. "That's why she'll come. And then you can apprehend her."

The apprehending Rebecca part he was in agreement with, but he was not at all happy at the thought of Sarah as the worm on the fishing hook. The fisherman might catch his quarry, but the worm never fared well in the process.

But he kept those thoughts to himself for the time being. Sarah wasn't wrong about Rebecca. "You would be there?" he asked Joanna.

"I promised my husband I'd return home to him, but I could be at the ball if you needed me. Perhaps I can persuade Michael to join me. I'm sure some of our associates would be happy to help out, too."

Hart smiled at that. The "associates" Joanna referred to were the other members of Wellington's intelligence gathering ring. Old Welly had only ever intended for them to gather information and pass it along to him, but as the war on the Peninsula raged, the members of the ring had become of necessity more independent. And this was exactly the kind of threat they'd come to handle on their own.

"Thorston would come down from the north of England, surely. And Fortescue is in and out of London on a regular basis," Hart said, ticking off the names on his fingers. Thorston already knew of the threat against Sarah, and Fortescue may have heard about it on one of his jaunts into Town. "Who else?"

"Wolf was planning to visit London the last time I saw him," Joanna replied. "He was interested in catching the London shop bomber. You might be able to convince Bannerman, but don't count on it. He seldom leaves his home now."

Bannerman in particular would be useful—he was an explosives expert. And Wolf was always ready to take a malefactor out of commission. Ollie would certainly lend a hand as well. If Joanna and her husband attended, that made seven trained fighters who would be watching over Sarah. And Hart would be at her side the whole evening.

"It could work."

"It *will* work," Sarah corrected.

MacDonald piped up, voicing Hart's own fear. "What if she brings her phosgene bombs? A spectacle like that, with all those people..."

"That's the beauty of it," Sarah smiled. "There won't be any guests. At least, not inside Elliott House. We'll hold the actual ball on another part of the property, an outbuilding that can be cleared and decorated in time, perhaps, or even outside. We'll have the guests come to the house as usual and usher them through. On the outside it will look as if everything is proceeding normally for a private ball at a large home, but the guests will be safely away from danger."

Hart grinned. His wife was absolutely brilliant. "And Rebecca can bring as many phosgene bombs as she'd like. Sarah knows how to decompose the gas."

MacDonald's brow creased. "Decompose?"

"Break it down into its components," Sarah supplied. "All we need is water and chalk."

"Chalk?" Hart repeated. "That's the base?"

She nodded. "I found it just before Richards directed me here."

Hart smiled, relieved. He'd nearly had to work a miracle to get the muriatic acid in such a short amount of time. "We can manage chalk."

"And a ball?"

He had no idea how they were going to host a ball to attract the attention of a mass murderer without endangering anyone. But it was a better idea than spending untold months looking for Rebecca, leaving her to wreak havoc across the realm and menace Sarah.

"We'll make it happen."

Sarah held his gaze for a moment that was both forever and the blink of an eye. Her smile faded, but her blue eyes were steady and she nodded once. "Then let's plan a ball."

MacDonald excused himself to his chamber looking slightly overwhelmed. Hart supposed if he had to travel for days with a stranger to inform on the woman who was to be his sister-in-law, he'd be a bit worse for the wear, too. Joanna elected to remain, and Hart left her with Sarah to work out the details of this unusual ball while he went to write the necessary letters to his housekeeper at Elliott House, to Ollie, and to his fellow intelligence ring members.

Sarah's first ball as Countess of Hartland and Diana wasn't here to help her plan it. It didn't matter that there might be other balls in the future. Sarah wished her best friend was sitting beside her, helping her choose flowers and refreshments and musicians.

Joanna proved to be both helpful and friendly, though. She'd also been to Elliott House, which was more than Sarah could say.

"So the carriages can wait here for the evening..." Joanna pointed to an area on the map she'd sketched of the grounds. "They'll be within sight of anyone arriving, and Hartland's stable lads can spend the evening patrolling in case someone hides something—or someone—undesirable in his or her vehicle."

"Good idea."

Joanna withdrew her hand from the sketch and turned her gaze on Sarah, tilting her head slightly. "Is there something you want to ask me?"

There were dozens of things Sarah wanted to ask this stranger who seemed to be part of the family. But she started with something easy. "Hartland said something about wanting me to meet you before today, but not to say anything about it in front of Mr. MacDonald. Do you know why?"

"Hart probably didn't want Mr. MacDonald to find out who I really am." Sarah must have looked confused because Joanna smiled. "Joanna Perkins is the name I use when I am in public, or with strangers."

"Strangers like me," Sarah added.

"Strangers like Mr. MacDonald," Joanna amended. "My work is sometimes of a sensitive nature, and not everyone needs to know my real name."

"Like Hartland and his Armored Man persona, if his identity was a secret."

Joanna laughed. "Yes, though I don't think his ego could handle a secret identity."

Sarah grinned. Before they were married, Hartland had never shied away from the spotlight even when he didn't actively seek it. "He's done reasonably well playing the new husband with me, though I know being away from Town in the middle of an investigation has worn on him."

"I'm sure it has."

"Hartland also said you were the Joanna he thought should teach me to shoot, but I don't think the name he used was Perkins."

"Devlin is my married name. Hartland thought I should teach you to shoot?"

Sarah clasped her hands together in her lap, recalling the day she'd rediscovered her courage and asked to learn to use a weapon. "I presume he's told you something of my situation or you wouldn't be here with Mr. MacDonald."

"He has."

"Did he mention the attack at Hartland Abbey?"

Joanna nodded slowly. "We only had a few minutes to talk before you arrived, but he told me about the ambush. Don't worry, he was discreet," she offered in response Sarah's raised eyebrows.

"He made sure Mr. MacDonald didn't overhear anything."

"Good." Hartland had only reluctantly allowed her to tell her own mother the truth. If he'd been careless in front of a complete stranger...

"He wouldn't do anything that could put you in more danger," Joanna replied. "He only told me because he thought I might be able to help. And I think he wanted some reassurance that he was indeed doing everything he could to keep you safe."

"Hartland needed reassurance?" Sarah tried to remember a time when he'd been anything except confident, but nothing sprung to mind.

"He seems rather unnerved by the whole thing." Joanna paused a moment, staring at the drawing of Elliott House. "I haven't seen him this concerned about anyone since Major Oliver's convalescence."

Sarah leaned forward slightly in her chair. "You were here when Major Oliver returned from Spain?"

"I was. Hartland was beside himself with worry, but he tried desperately to hide it. He buried himself in his workshop for days at a time, working on various suits of armor for soldiers to wear in battle. He pushed himself past the point his body could endure and ended up confined to bed himself for several days."

Joanna paused again, tilting her head slightly to one side. "But when he told me what happened at Hartland Abbey, he didn't even try to disguise how afraid he'd been. I don't think he could have, anyway. It's plain as the nose on his handsome face that he loves you."

Even with her resentment of Hartland and his decisions *for her own good*, her traitorous heart danced a happy jig at Joanna's pronouncement. Sarah's conflicting emotions must have shown on her face, because Joanna gave her a small smile.

"He did something foolish, didn't he?"

"Yes." She was willing to concede that much, but the rest was between husband and wife. "He's promised to make it up to me, and has so far been as good as his word."

"But it was enormously stupid and you aren't sure you want to forgive him yet."

Sarah noticed that Joanna's words were a statement rather than a question. Perhaps Joanna knew Hartland as well as Sarah did—or better. "It's not so much that I don't want to forgive him. It's that I'm not sure I can forget how much he hurt me."

Joanna smiled again, and this time the gesture included a note of pain. "I'm no expert on marriage, but I have a bit of experience in asking forgiveness of one's spouse. If he truly loves you, he will remember the consequences of this thing he's done and he'll try his damnedest to keep from doing it again."

If that were the case, perhaps Sarah might be able to let go of her anger. She would never forget what Hart had done, but if she could believe he actually saw her as a person with her own mind rather than a fatuous female to be coddled, there might yet be hope. Unless, of course, he still wanted his own life separate from hers.

"Do you think so?"

"I do."

Well, that was something worth considering. Did Hartland love her? He'd never said so, but words were not the only way to express one's feelings.

"I also think teaching you to shoot is a good idea, particularly since Hartland tends to carry pistols when he's likely to be in danger. If we can find twenty minutes together, I'll show you how to handle one."

Sarah nodded. Perhaps another frank conversation with her husband was in order. Though probably not while she was holding a loaded gun.

Chapter Fourteen

THE RETURN JOURNEY to London was just as tedious as the drive to Devon had been, though the sea crossing had at least allowed them to be on deck enjoying the sun and the salt breeze. Hart had considered riding alongside the carriage on horseback once they reached land again, but vetoed the idea almost immediately. After the attack at Hartland Abbey and the murder of Lady Ashfield, there was no way he was letting Sarah out of his sight while they were vulnerable on the road. He had acceded to her wish not to travel through the night this time, but countered with a full complement of footmen to serve as guards. Richards rode up on the box with the coachman as both a lookout and an extra set of hands should trouble find them.

They would not be caught unawares again.

But riding inside a carriage with a woman who no longer tolerates your presence is disheartening, to say the least. And while Hart was sure the scenery was, in fact, changing beyond his window, he seemed to see the same field every time he looked out and the same herd of red cows. If he could focus long enough he'd read, but his eyes kept wandering to his wife.

She sat in the rear-facing seat, leaning against the carriage wall and ignoring the book in her lap to stare out of her own window. The sun shone on her hair, marking out blonde and red strands among the brown. Was she thinking about their marriage? Afraid of another attack? Wondering why she saw the same four sheep over and over?

"Sarah, may I tell you a story?"

She dragged her eyes from the window and turned them on him. "What kind of a story?"

"A personal one."

If she reacted, he didn't see it. He lifted his brows in an unasked question and tilted his head.

"Perhaps it will help pass the time," she said, nodding.

"You once asked me why I built different types of armor and chose to use them to protect people."

She sat up a little straighter. "I did."

"It started when Ollie was sent to the Continent a few years ago." Hart shifted in his seat, unable to get comfortable. "Well, you've seen how I cope with stress."

"You went into your workshop," she said with a small smile.

Hart leaned back against the velvet seat, lacing his fingers together and resting them on his abdomen. "I've always been one for making things, and when Ollie went to war I became particularly interested in making things that would keep soldiers safe in battle."

"Why armor?"

She seemed genuinely interested in his answer, and that pleased Hart more than he'd expected it to. "What could protect a body better than being covered from head to toe in steel?" he grinned. "I knew that armor had become practically useless as firearms became more accurate and more powerful, but I thought I could improve upon the old designs."

"I remember you telling me that the first time you showed me a brigandine."

When they'd waltzed around his workshop at Hartland Abbey as the rain poured down outside. That was a day he'd likely never forget—if he hadn't been in love with Sarah before then, he certainly was afterward. He'd pushed the emotion down that day in order to focus on solving the mystery of her death threat, but he hadn't been able to deny its existence.

And he no longer wanted to.

"I drew up all sorts of designs, and built most of them, trying to get the most protection and the best mobility out of one suit. I wanted... I *needed* to do everything in my power to protect the only family I had."

"Of course you did." Her voice was soft, knowing.

He loved that she understood him. Even Ollie, who'd known him longer than anyone else, had never fully grasped Hart's motivations. But more often than not, Sarah did.

"I think that's why I was so keen to save you," he confessed quietly. "You once told me that it would be easier to send you away somewhere while I stayed in London to sort out the problem. But I couldn't do it. After Ollie and Richards you were the closest thing I had to a real friend, and I thought you'd be safest with me. Turns out I was wrong, but I did try."

She leaned forward and laid a hand on his knee. "You weren't wrong. If not for you I'd likely be dead by now. I'd have been all on my own with no idea how to deal with danger when it came for me, and I would have had my mother to worry about, too. You've kept us both safe."

The warmth from her hand permeated his trousers and shot up to his heart...with a short detour through his manhood. He fought not to close his eyes and savor the sensation. She'd barely touched him since their falling out; the contact now sent frissons of pleasure through both organs.

Instead, he sat up and clasped her hand in his larger one, bringing her fingers to his mouth for a kiss. "I would do anything for you. You know that, don't you?"

"I do." Her voice was even as she spoke, and her lips curved into a small smile. "That's part of what makes it so difficult to remain angry with you."

"Then don't."

It was his usual blunt response delivered with his usual grin, but her own smile faded. "Would that it were so easy. Perhaps I'm not even angry any longer, Hartland, but I don't trust you. Not with my heart."

For a single second he thought she said "my Hart," and another bolt of pleasure ran through his body. When her actual words registered a moment later, the pleasure drained away and left the sting of disappointment in its place. Hart leaned forward and reached for her free hand, holding both her hands over their nearly-touching knees. He absolutely hated baring his soul like this, but the urge to make amends with his wife far outweighed any emotional discomfort he felt.

"I have badly bungled our relationship, and I can't even promise I'll never do it again." He chuckled to cover the nervousness that suddenly surged through him, running his thumbs over the back of her hands to steady himself. "In fact, I can almost promise that I *will* do it again. But I can learn from my mistakes, and I can promise never to make the same one twice."

"Promises to earn back my trust, to learn from your mistakes, and to never make the same mistake twice. I'm going to hold you to those."

Her voice was steady, her body relatively relaxed. She wasn't angry, then, but neither was she smiling. She likely needed time to consider his words, and quite probably her own feelings. As much as he wanted her to throw her arms around him right then and kiss him all the way to London, he reminded himself to be patient. If he forced her hand she would close herself off from him again, and Hart didn't think he could deal with that pain a second time.

He contented himself by dropping another kiss on her hands before releasing them. "I expect nothing less."

The news appeared in all the gossip rags even before the Hartlands had even returned to Town. The first ball at Elliott House hosted by the current earl was to be held in a week's time, and everyone was waiting with breathless anticipation.

They're trying to draw you out, the paper said to her as she read it. *They will be ready for you.*

"Of course they will," she replied aloud, throwing it down on the old table at which she sat. She couldn't afford to be in her parents' house for more than a few minutes—a reward had been offered for information on her whereabouts, and she doubted the servants in the neighboring houses would hesitate to turn her in. But she'd returned for the supply of black powder her father had kept for his pistols, and had wandered about the house one last time, touching each piece of furniture beneath the sheets protecting them from light and dust.

She was so tired from running. How lovely it would be to live in the house again, to have servants and clean clothing and her own hair color once more. To retake her place in society as the daughter of an earl.

She'd sat down at the dining table to read those horrid gossip rags and pretend for just a moment that things were as they used to be. She'd tried to forget that she'd found the papers abandoned on the street several days after they'd been printed, instead of sending a servant to purchase them when the news was still fresh. She'd hoped to find out where Lord Hartland and his misbegotten wife were, and had been slapped in the face with this celebration of their marriage.

Rebecca knew they were trying to control her final assault on Sarah, trying to force her to come to a place familiar to them where they could prepare defensive measures. It was the only logical explanation for having such a public gathering after hiding for weeks.

But she didn't care.

The Hartlands might think that they had an advantage by luring her to their own home.

They didn't.

Lord Hartland and his murdering wife had no idea what was in store for them.

Sarah sat down on the bed and looked about her bedchamber for a place to keep the tiny pistol Joanna had lent her for the journey back to London. She had been given the best room in the inn, and while everything appeared very clean, the furnishings were rather sparse. Not liking the idea of having a loaded firearm under her pillow, Sarah laid it on the floor beside the head of her bed. It was close enough to be easily reached in the event she needed it, but she didn't have to worry about setting it off in her sleep.

She stared at the little gun a moment longer. She'd become competent enough at hitting trees at Glanmire House, but would she be able to shoot straight under pressure? How would it feel to shoot an actual person if she had to? Could she live with herself if she took another life?

What she needed was reassurance. Lucy had already undressed her for the night, but Sarah dug a wrapper out of her luggage and put it on over her nightgown. She peeked out the door before exiting, nodding at the two footmen in bright Hartland red that had been posted outside as her personal guard. Stepping around them, she sidled up to the next door and knocked hesitantly.

"Enter."

His back was to the door when she opened it, his body bare except for the trousers he wore. She longed to run her hands over his skin and to have his hands on her, to strip off his trousers and her nightclothes and feel the pleasure she knew he could give her, and to give him pleasure in return. But until she knew if she could trust him with her heart, physical intimacy would only complicate matters.

"Hartland."

He turned and his eyebrows shot up. "Sarah." He cleared his throat and schooled his features. When he spoke again, it was in a lower register. "I didn't expect to see you again tonight."

"I didn't either," she allowed. Then, since he had been making a point to be honest with her, she offered up some honesty of her own. "I-I was frightening myself, thinking of all the awful things that could happen in the next few days. Would you talk to me for a while? Help me settle my nerves?"

"Of course." He gestured for her to sit on his bed, then picked his shirt up off the floor and pulled it on over his head. "What would you like to talk about?"

"Anything," she responded automatically. "No, wait. There is something I'd actually like to discuss."

He raised his eyebrows again and tilted his head slightly to one side, seating himself next to her.

She'd become bold in the bedchamber and in anger. But boldness in the calmness of a normal conversation seemed a much bigger leap. Taking a deep breath and letting it out slowly, she looked down at her hands folded in her lap. "We haven't talked about the possibility of a non-aristocratic marriage."

"A non-aristocratic marriage?"

Was he confused or just disbelieving? She forced her gaze to meet his. "What if I didn't want to lead a life separate from yours after all this is over? I'm not saying that *is* what I want," she added quickly. "But more information is better when making important decisions."

"What would you like to know?"

His expression was neutral, his voice even. Did he really not care if she stayed with him or not? "What would it be like? How would it work?"

"We would stay mostly at Elliott House, I think. My Armored Man activities center around London and its surroundings because that seems to be where I'm most needed."

That certainly wouldn't be a hardship. Sarah had lived her entire life in Town, and Elliott House in Hampstead was near enough to almost seem like she still did. "What else?"

"You would have charge of the house and the servants, and I'd expect you to do the same at all my properties."

Sarah nodded. That she'd expected. If she were to remain with Hartland, she would need to take on the duties of a countess and mistress of his households.

"You might also take part in the entertainments of the Season if you wish, though I would probably beg you not to offer up our home to guests very often."

He grinned as he spoke the last and she found herself smiling in response. "If there is one thing I've learned from this ordeal with Lady Rebecca, it's how much work goes into planning a ball." She'd learned so much more in the weeks since she'd first learned of the threat against her, of course, but it felt good to be the one making quips for a change.

He obliged her and chuckled. "Exactly so."

An awkward silence descended upon them and Hart cleared his throat. "You did say that you wanted to become a mother—that could also be arranged."

She'd called her children her legacy the day she married Hartland, and still looked forward to bringing them into the world if she were so blessed. She might, even now, be carrying Hart's child, and her cheeks warmed as she recalled the night they had spent in his bed. "I-I would like that."

"Raising the children or making them?" he winked.

Was it her imagination, or was he breathing a bit faster? She certainly was. "Both," she confessed, smiling despite the redness she knew was collecting on her face.

He reached for her, but yanked his hand back before he touched her. "I thought you enjoyed our night together. Would you still, though, if you hated me?"

"Oh, Hartland, I never hated you." She slid closer to him on the bed and took his hand. "I was very angry with you, certainly. And mistrustful. And hurt. But I never hated you."

His shoulders relaxed visibly. "That's good to hear."

She leaned forward and dropped a kiss on his shoulder. It was meant more to reassure him than anything, but her aim was a little off and her lips connected with his skin instead of linen. Her heart joined her lungs in increasing its tempo while a compulsion built inside her to kiss him again. For once, she let her body win out over her brain and pressed her lips to his neck.

His hand caressed her cheek, her hair, guiding her face to his. She opened her mouth in anticipation and was rewarded when his mouth covered hers. The kiss was firm but not forceful, tender without being hesitant. She moaned, sliding even closer to him on the bed and wrapping her arms around him. She had missed this—missed *him*—and savored the feel of him against her.

When his hand slipped inside her wrapper, though, she broke away. Her body screamed at her to continue, to give and receive the pleasure she knew would come. But her cautiousness won the day and she rose from the bed, taking several steps away.

"You still don't trust me," he said, a note of impatience entering his voice.

She didn't blame him for feeling frustrated. In his place, Sarah would be questioning everything she'd done over the past weeks and wondering what more she could possibly do.

"I can't help it," was all she managed to say. Pulling her wrapper more tightly around her, she turned toward his door. "I'll return to my chamber. Good night, Hartland."

Sarah fumbled with the door for a moment, but managed to extract herself without looking back at her husband. Nor did she look at the footmen outside her own door even as one opened it for her. She closed it behind her and leaned against the sturdy oak for a long time, attempting to calm her body.

When she finally felt somewhat composed once again, she shed her wrapper and dropped onto her bed, leaning back against the headboard. Well, she wasn't frightened any longer, but her conversation with Hartland hadn't exactly soothed her into drowsiness.

The muted sounds of a scuffle in the corridor drifted through the thin walls. Some gentleman in his cups? Hartland sparring with Richards? A distraction to lure her guards away from her chamber?

Her door rattled as if something had been thrown against it and a male voice groaned. She wrapped her arms around herself. What was going on out there?

The door burst open and two loud *bang*s echoed against the bare walls. Sarah instinctively curled into a ball and covered her head as splinters of wood burst from the headboard mere inches from her shoulder.

Heavy boots thudded across her chamber and she scrambled off the bed, her only objective to get away from this new threat. She moved as fast as she could, but her nightgown tangled in her legs and impeded her escape. Two metallic *thump*s hit her ears and the heavy steps tracked her across the floor. Where were the footmen who were supposed to protect her?

"Hartl—"

She screamed his name as loud as she could, but her cry was cut off midway by a hand squeezing her throat. Another hand joined the first, slamming her against the wall and pinning her there. She clawed at the hands, trying desperately to remember what Hart had taught her. Feet.

Something about feet...stepping on feet? Stomping on feet!

She lifted one foot and brought it down with all her strength, but she was barefoot and her assailant was wearing heavy boots. He flinched, but recovered quickly and redoubled his effort to strangle her.

Sarah heard a dull *thunk* and her assailant grunted. Then, just as quickly as he'd dominated her he released her.

She opened her eyes, only then realizing that she'd closed them, and gasped for air. Her attacker was still standing, but had turned his attention to another party in the room.

"Hartland!" she croaked painfully. He stood in the center of her chamber, an unfastened brigandine draped over his shoulders, holding a pistol by its long barrel. The butt had blood on it.

"Run, Sarah!"

She tried desperately to make her legs work, but her body refused to obey. She slumped to the floor, tears streaming down her face as her chest heaved. Hart and the assailant were grunting, each throwing punches in an effort to subdue the other. The assailant's punches were measured, strategically placed on Hart's face, chest, and body, where he wasn't protected by the brigandine. Hart, on the other hand, was swinging ferociously, connecting enough times to make his opponent stagger back a step.

But not enough to knock him out.

Sarah got to her hands and knees, crawling around the perimeter of the room toward her bed. If she could get behind Hart, he would literally shield her from further attack and she could reach Joanna's pocket-sized pistol. Her pace was agonizingly slow, but her limbs felt heavier than the boxes of books that used to arrive at her parents' shop and just as difficult to move. She was gasping and coughing with the effort, but Hart was losing ground to the larger attacker and she couldn't stop now.

After what seemed an age, she finally reached the head of her bed. The pistol wasn't where she left it and for one terrifying moment she thought she and Hart were both going to die in this little inn. Then she spotted the gun under the bed and lunged for it. Turning over onto her back she took aim, using her remaining energy to hold her arms steady and pull the trigger.

The tang of burning gunpowder filled her nose and her arms dropped to the floor. Had she hit him? Was he dead? Was Hart? She had no strength left to lift her head and look.

"Sarah?"

Hart was bending over her, his roughened hand caressing her face, his brown eyes wide with fear.

"Hartland," she whispered. She managed a smile to reassure him before her eyes drifted closed.

She felt arms slid beneath her, lifting her off the floor and placing her gently on the bed. "Fetch a physician!" Hart yelled at someone. To her he said softly, "Where are you hurt?"

"Throat." It was barely a word, but he seemed to understand.

"Anywhere else?"

She shook her head ever so slightly. Her hands and knees were sore from crawling, but that was a minor concern.

She opened her eyes as he sat down beside her, leaning over her to inspect her neck. The grimace on his face told her everything she needed to know about her condition. His wasn't much better—bruises were beginning to form on his cheek and one eye, his shirt was torn and bloody beneath his open brigandine. Whether it was his own blood or his opponent's, Sarah couldn't tell. But he was whole and alive, and when he held her hand against his chest she could feel his heart beating against her palm.

"Footmen?"

Hart shook his head. "Dead. Both stabbed."

"Is he…?"

She tried to point her chin toward the man on the floor, and Hart glanced back at him. "He's alive. Wounded, but alive."

"How bad…?"

"How badly is he wounded?" When she nodded, Hart turned again. Richards was binding their assailant while the innkeeper pressed a towel to his back. "Looks like your shot struck somewhere near his shoulder blade. And there's an ugly gash where I hit him with the butt of his own pistol—he was courteous enough to leave two of them on the floor for me."

She was too exhausted to contemplate what that meant for the mortality of the man who'd tried to kill her, too drained even to cry. Her fingers curled around Hart's and her eyes closed again. She knew he'd see to her care and comfort, and to the man being dragged from her chamber.

He bowed his head against her shoulder and took in a shaky breath. "If I had been half a minute later..."

She summoned an energy reserve she didn't realize she had and loosened her hand from his, wrapping him in her arms. He reciprocated, carefully raising her from her pillow to hold her close.

"You weren't," she whispered. That's when the tears came, bringing with them big, racking sobs that tore at her throat. Hart held her tighter, cradling her head with one hand, his face pressed to her shoulder.

Later, when the physician had come and gone, prescribing rest and as little talking as possible for a few days, Lucy helped her change into a fresh nightgown. The one she'd been wearing was torn where it had caught on a nail during her odyssey across the chamber floor, and Hart had transferred some of the blood on him to her. Lucy slipped the clean nightgown over Sarah's head and bundled up the soiled one at the end of the bed to discard later. As she strode to the other side of the room to lay out her mistress's clothing for the morning, Sarah let her gaze drift to the damaged nightgown.

Among the rips and the blood where two small, slightly damp patches on the shoulder of the gown.

Chapter Fifteen

THEY TRAVELED AROUND the clock after the attack at the inn, stopping only to change horses and refresh themselves. Hart knew it was uncomfortable for Sarah, knew that she didn't sleep well in the carriage as it rattled along the bumpy roads. But they were safer if they kept moving. Twice now he'd failed to protect her and she'd nearly died.

He would not fail her a third time.

She convalesced for another day after they reached Elliott House, but then insisted she could handle preparations for the ball. He acquiesced, hoping the activity would keep her from dwelling on the attack. When Joanna arrived, he breathed both a metaphorical and literal sigh of relief. In her work as a spy for Wellington, Joanna had been to many a ball and could be Sarah's voice when her own became weak.

Hart remained with her as often as possible, unwilling to let her out of his sight. He even began slipping into her bedchamber at night, relieving her maid to sit with Sarah as she slept, climbing into her bed and holding her close when nightmares made her cry out.

His own injuries looked worse than they were —a couple of cracked ribs and a broken finger hidden beneath an assortment of bruises. Their assailant had been well-controlled during the attack, but Hart had been able to block some of the punches thrown his way. He didn't even care about the ones that had connected. He'd heal, and the pain felt like penance for allowing Sarah to be half-strangled.

They ended up with fourteen guests who had been told the real reason for Hart's ball, ten of whom were trained fighters. Wolf had declined Hart's invitation to take care of his own business, so he wouldn't be participating. And Hugh Bannerman wouldn't be fighting anyone, having only agreed to come out of his self-imposed seclusion to rig the fireworks show Sarah had requested. But the others in Wellington's intelligence gathering ring were willing and able to do what was needed when the time came.

Four ladies temporarily joined the team, too. None of them officially knew about the ring—though Hart suspected they knew more than they were supposed to—but were all either married or betrothed to one of its members. They'd volunteered to help in whatever way they could, and had in turn been given the details of the threat against Sarah.

They were all gathered together in Hart's library, with the exception of Bannerman, sipping after-dinner port or tea two days before the ball, brimming with questions about their roles in the apprehension of the London shop bomber.

"Where do you want me to be?"

"What shall I do?"

"What does this Lady Rebecca look like?"

"Will she bring bombs to the ball?"

"What do we do if she brings other weapons?"

Hart held up his hands to quiet the room. "Perhaps this would be a good time for Lady Hartland to explain her plan."

An eyebrow or two was raised, but after working with a very capable Joanna for the past four years, Hart figured the surprise was due more to the fact that the men from Wellington's intelligence gathering ring had never met Sarah before this night. She stood, her pale yellow gown with delicate lace on the hem and sleeves reinforcing the notion that she was a typical aristocratic female.

"For anyone not in this room, this ball should be exactly what they expect. There will be dancing, refreshments, a card room, and torches at the back of the outbuilding to light the way for anyone seeking a reprieve from the crowd. Mr. Bannerman is putting together a fireworks display that guests will be able to watch from the lawn. Then we go to work."

Hart noted that the eyebrows had returned to their resting state, and all eyes were on Sarah. She managed to speak with authority without raising her voice past the limit the physician had set or resorting to the quips and puns he tended to employ, holding the attention of each person in the room. Not one pair of eyes wandered toward the clock on the mantel, nor did one hand pick at a loose thread.

"Based on what my husband has told me about everyone, I've devised assignments for each of you. We'll go through the plan here, then take up our positions and rehearse a little to make sure everyone is clear on their part."

She turned to her left and nodded to the archer in the group. "Mr. Hoskins, you will be our lookout for the evening. We have a ladder long enough to reach the lower roof on either wing of the house, and you may choose your perch from any place you can reach. I'll give you a full description of your quarry, and you'll blow this whistle—" Sarah handed Hoskins a silver-plated whistle that had belonged to Hart's father. "—when she is within sight. The earlier the warning, the better."

"Sounds like a lovely evening," Hoskins answered, accepting the small instrument with a smile. "We should have torches along the front drive as well for better viewing."

"Already ordered," Sarah nodded. "Lord Adam St. Peters and Miss Watson, you will join Mr. Hoskins as lookouts. One of you will be positioned at the foot of the drive, one a short distance down the road. Be sure to stay close enough to each other to hear the whistles. The more eyes we have watching, the better our chances are of spotting her before she does any damage."

She handed whistles to Miss Watson and St. Peters, who accepted them with a glance at each other. St Peters looked a mite worried, and Hart sympathized with the man. It couldn't have been easy to watch his recently betrothed put herself potentially in harm's way. Miss Watson, though, was grinning.

"Lord Thorston and Mr. Devlin, you are charged with perimeter security—it will be up to you keep Lady Rebecca from entering the house. She could arrive alone or with any number of companions, so you'll need to be alert. If you cannot apprehend her, or them, then at the very least you will need to delay their entry as long as possible. Hartland has handpicked a small group of footmen to accompany you and help cover more ground."

Thorston exchanged glances with his assigned partner, then turned his attention back to Sarah. "You may rely upon us."

"Good," Hart interjected. The ferocious scowl Thorston wore and the stony expression on Devlin's face were proof enough that they understood what was at stake, but Hart said it anyway. "Because if Rebecca or anyone she's working with gets inside this house, Sarah's life is in real danger."

Silence hung in the air for a brief moment before Sarah continued. "Major Oliver and Captain Alexander, you two will act as a second line of defense inside the house with your own contingent of handpicked footmen. If Lady Rebecca or any of her associates make it into the house, it will be your job to stop her."

The two military men nodded their assent to Sarah, no doubt planning strategies in their minds already.

"Miss Hale and Mrs. Hoskins," Sarah continued, "Your task will be to stay with our guests in the outbuilding in the event Rebecca discovers our relocation of the ball. I am her primary target, but she has already demonstrated that she will kill and injure others as well, so you will need to be on the lookout for anything unusual."

Miss Atwell had mentioned earlier that Mrs. Hoskins was also an excellent fighter, and Hart approved of the choice to keep her with the crowd. It built in another layer of protection should someone with bad intentions get past the rest of the security measures.

"That's what the fireworks show is for, isn't it?" Mrs. Hoskins asked. "So we have something to distract the guests?"

"Exactly," Sarah replied. "Lord Adam Bateman, Mr. Bannerman will need assistance with the fireworks. He will have the materials already prepared, but the display he has planned requires more than one person."

Bateman frowned slightly, as if he'd hoped for a different assignment. Hart probably would have been disappointed, too, to be stuck outside away from the action. But the show Bannerman had designed really did require more than one set of hands, and Bateman could also help to keep his friend's notorious temper in check. They couldn't afford a raging Bannerman in addition to the threat Rebecca already posed.

"Miss Atwell and Mrs. Perkins, you are tasked with my personal safety. Hartland and I disagreed about how much protection I needed," she sent a wry smile his way, and he responded with his signature grin. Hart had tried to insist on a dozen guards until she'd revealed her choices. "But I believe your physical skills will be excellent assets."

"We will make sure you are unharmed," Miss Atwell said, and Hart knew she meant it. He'd never seen her fight, but if Alexander was to be believed, his fiancée could more than handle herself if the evening got rough.

"That leaves Hartland and Mr. Fortescue," Sarah continued. "You two will be on phosgene cleanup duty if any of the gas is released. All you'll need to handle is water and chalk, but phosgene is dangerous and so is the muriatic acid that is produced when it breaks down. Hartland has protective clothing you both can wear, and the staff working inside the house have orders to open all windows when given the signal."

Hart's grin faded. He'd much rather have been in the thick of things, protecting his wife or guarding the metaphorical gates. But his injuries from the attack at the inn curtailed his physical participation. Ridding the house of any phosgene that might be unleashed, though, was an important assignment, one Sarah had wanted to handle herself. But no one could be sure how or when Rebecca might release the gas, and Sarah might be too busy trying to stay alive herself to worry about a house full of poison.

"Is everyone clear on their duties?"

Heads nodded all around the room, including Hart's. He reminded himself that it was a solid plan and a formidable group executing it, that even if they couldn't foresee every possibility, they would adapt to whatever situation presented itself. But he couldn't shake the fear that gripped his heart.

Sarah surveyed her troops. The expression on her face was one of satisfaction, but when Hart looked more closely he could see her hands shaking.

Sarah sat at the escritoire in her chamber after everyone else had gone to bed, reading the letters the Marquess of Thorston had brought from her mother. Mrs. Shipton complained a little of the weather, that periodic storms were keeping her confined to the house. But she spent paragraphs describing Lord Thorston's care of her, how he devised entertainments for her and escorted her any time she wanted to leave the estate. She mentioned missing Sarah and wanting to get to know her new son-in-law, but overall she seemed to be in good spirits. Lord Thorston had kept his word; Mrs. Shipton was safe.

A knock sounded at her door and Sarah jumped. She'd put on a calm, cool exterior for her guests earlier in the evening, relieved for the chance to work and plan and push the danger from her mind. But after the attack at the inn, she wasn't sure if she'd ever feel truly safe and settled again.

"Come in."

The door swung open and Hartland stepped inside, no longer wearing the tailcoat he'd donned for the gathering in the library, but still clad in his waistcoat, shirt, and trousers. He shut the door carefully behind him and made his way over to her, coming to a halt a couple of feet from her chair.

"Are you all right?"

Sarah blinked and realized she had unshed tears in her eyes. Her emotions were still too close to the surface for her liking after the last attack. She wiped the tears away with the back of her hand. "I was just reading letters from my mother that Lord Thorston was kind enough to carry. I suppose I missed her more than I realized."

Hartland reached out and stroked her shoulder. "Thorston swears she's hale and hearty."

"She is," Sarah replied, covering his hand with one of hers. "And she sounds as if she's enjoying herself. I will have to thank him for his diligence and generosity."

"I already have, but I suspect he'd be much more receptive to you." Hart winked, then turned his hand over under hers and curled his fingers around her palm. "I've come to ask you a favor. No, make that two favors."

His voice was low, almost soft. What could he want from her? "Ask what you will."

"Is there any way I can talk you out of attending the ball tomorrow night? I can have a carriage ready in minutes to take you anywhere you might want to go."

He probably had his best coachman already waiting. "You know I can't. There's no telling what Rebecca will do if I'm not there, and I will not put the lives of you and your friends at more risk than they already are."

"But you would be safe."

She shook her head, turning her body toward his. "Maybe safe for a while, but not for good."

"Safe for a while is better than dead tomorrow." His words were practically whispered, and there was no sign of his usual grin or sarcasm now. "I promised to protect you, and letting you walk into the arms of a murderer is no form of protection I've ever heard of."

"I have my armored stays, the fiercest guards in the realm, your 'associates,' and a solid plan," she reminded him gently. Part of her wanted to be irritated with him for even asking her to abandon her plan, but the worry was etched plainly onto his face. This wasn't Hartland imposing his will upon her, it was her husband concerned for her safety. "I also have the skills you taught me, in addition to my strapping husband. I will be better protected than the Prince Regent tomorrow night."

He pressed his lips together, then raised her to her feet and slid his arms around her. "Yes you will."

She wrapped her arms around his neck and pressed her cheek to his. His solid body against hers fortified her, giving her strength she badly needed despite all her declarations to the contrary. Walking into the arms of a murderer, as he put it, scared her more than anything.

She kissed his cheek and started to draw away. "What was the second favor you wanted to ask?"

Hart cinched his arms around her waist and held her in place. "I'd like you to come to bed with me."

Though they had occasionally shared a bed after the attack at the inn, Sarah had mixed feelings about doing so now. The previous occasions had happened out Sarah's need for comfort in the night. This time it would be a decision made with a clear head. "Hartland..."

"We don't have to do anything but sleep," he added quickly. "You don't even have to touch me if you don't want to. I will simply sleep better knowing you are safe and sound beside me. I thought perhaps you might, too."

There was no question that sleeping next to Hart would ease Sarah's fears. But was that merely because of the physical danger she was in? Or had she fallen in love with her husband? "I don't know..."

He cupped her face in one large hand. "Just for tonight. Not only did I promise to protect you, but I promised you an aristocratic marriage. Once Rebecca Barrington is taken into custody you will never have to see me again if you don't want to."

Never see him again? Sarah wasn't sure she wanted that, but they didn't need to decide that issue now. "For tonight, then. I will sleep better with you nearby."

"Good." He pressed a lingering kiss to her temple, then released her. "Shall I send in your maid? Or do you want more time with your letters?"

"I told her to come up at midnight. I'll come to bed then." That gave Sarah ten more minutes to read her mother's letters, and to decide what to wear to bed—a concern she'd never had before, but suddenly seemed important.

Hart left her alone and Sarah's mind raced like an out-of-control carriage. The plan she'd put in place was a good one, and so were the people Hart had asked to help implement it. But it was entirely possible that this was her last night among the living. How did she want to spend it?

She settled on an old nightgown that she'd worn a hundred times before her marriage and slipped into Hart's bedchamber after dismissing Lucy for the night. He was already lying in bed, clad in a nightshirt with the sheet pulled up to his waist and his hands tucked behind his head.

Sarah climbed into the big bed with him, pulling the sheet up over herself and stretching out on her side facing him. "Do you ever regret marring me?" she asked quietly.

"Never," he answered without hesitation. He turned slowly onto his good side and reached for her hand. "Not for one second."

"Truly? You wouldn't be happier without Rebecca and her bombs and threats and the rabid dogs she's sent after me?"

"Life would have been easier without all that, certainly." He slid closer to her and kissed her palm. "But I did promise to take you for better or for worse."

And he'd kept his promises—every one he had ever made to her. "You wouldn't have had to take me at all if not for the 'worse'," she reminded him.

"In that regard, I'm indebted to Rebecca Barrington," he chuckled. "I would never have thought to wed you if I hadn't compromised you trying to warn you of her threat. But it turned out to be the best thing I've ever done."

"Even if it kills you?"

"Even then."

He was an insensitive knave at times, but Sarah's heart was nearly bursting with tenderness for the man lying beside her. Not only had he literally saved her life more than once, but even when he had withheld information from her, he'd had her best interests in mind. And, most importantly, when she objected to his behavior, he'd changed it simply because she'd asked it of him.

"Hart, will you make love to me tonight?"

He didn't respond right away, but slipped his arm around her and pulled her to him. "Is that what you really want? Or do you think it's what I want?"

"Both," she smiled, running her fingers through his wavy hair. "I want you to make me forget about everything but the two of us and this bed, and I suspect you would be happy to oblige."

He levered himself over her carefully in deference to his damaged ribs, kissing her slowly and sliding a hand down her body. She wrapped her arms around him and kissed him back, her heart beating a staccato rhythm as she waiting for his hand to find bare skin. She broke away and sighed when he found the hem of her nightgown and began to draw it upward, caressing her hip, her belly, her breast.

He trailed kisses across her cheek and down her neck, pausing near her ear to whisper, "I love you, Sarah Elliott."

They shed their clothing and Sarah thought no more of his declaration, dismissing it as a product of the moment and concentrating instead on the physical pleasure he gave her. They were mindful of his injuries and her bruises, and when they'd exhausted themselves, they curled up together to find what sleep they might. She waited for his breathing to slow and become regular, for his body to relax against hers, before murmuring her own declaration.

"I love you, my Hart."

Chapter Sixteen

SARAH STOOD BESIDE her husband at the entrance to Elliott House's ballroom, with Joanna and Miss Atwell filling out the receiving line. There hadn't been time to have a new gown made for the occasion, so she'd chosen the green and silver gown she'd worn the day she married Hartland. He'd presented her with a parure of garnets, too, before they joined the others: drop earrings, a brooch, and rope necklace, all set in gold and trimmed with seed pearls. The gold jewelry didn't exactly complement the silver of her dress, but Sarah didn't care. The pieces were gifts from the man she loved, commissioned especially for her to match her wedding ring, and she would wear them with pride no matter the color of her clothing.

Hartland was likewise attired in spotless eveningwear, his shirt and cravat starkly white in contrast to the chocolate brown of his tailcoat. Sarah had dug through her belongings and found her father's gold watch fob, complete with tiny gold books dangling from the chain. She'd attached it herself to Hart's pocket, and it glinted in the candlelight from the chandeliers.

Guests were met at the front door by Richards, who compared their invitations to a list of invitees. A few people arrived hoping to gain entry without invitations, but they were all turned away without incident. The successful guests were escorted to the ballroom and announced by the butler to the waiting Hartlands. They were then ushered through the ballroom and out the French windows to the outbuilding where the festivities were actually being held. There were plenty of odd looks and Sarah knew it would be the one thing everyone talked about tomorrow. But having all those people two hundred yards away from the house kept them safer, and that was worth every moment of the social awkwardness to come.

When the steady stream of guests became more sporadic, Hartland reached for Sarah's hand and held it in both of his. "There's a chance she won't come tonight."

"She'll come."

He raised his dark brows. "What makes you so sure? She has to know we're waiting for her."

Sarah stepped closer and lowered her voice. "If someone took you from me, took away our future together, I'd want revenge."

Joanna and Miss Atwell had the courtesy to look away, pretending they weren't witnessing a private moment between husband and wife, but Sarah no longer cared if the entire world knew how she felt about Hart. She was only sorry it had taken the imminent possibility of her death to recognize it herself.

"You wouldn't act on it, though," Hartland replied. "Would you?"

"I'd like to think not. But I don't know how I would go on without you." She brought his hands to her lips and kissed them. "I dearly hope that tonight is not the night I have to find out."

He slid his arms around her and pulled her close without even a glance at their audience. "Living without you has been the theme of my nightmares these past weeks. I will not let tonight be the night they come true."

It still wasn't "I love you," but from a man like Hart it was as close as she was likely going to get when he was clear-headed. Nor did she need the exact words, she realized. She only needed him.

She wasn't sure who kissed whom, but they were interrupted too soon when Joanna cleared her throat. "Hoskins is blowing his whistle."

Their man stationed on the rooftop had sighted something suspicious. Sarah smoothed her husband's hair and pressed another kiss to his lips. "Here we go."

"You have your fan with you?"

He'd made her a beautiful fan with blades of sharpened steel, decorated with pearls to match her jewelry. It dangled from her wrist as if it were any other accessory, ready when she needed it. He didn't have to ask her about her armored stays, though—he'd laced her into those himself.

"I do, though I'd rather not have to use it." Using it meant that Rebecca was within an arm's length of Sarah's body, and she didn't want that woman coming anywhere near her.

Hartland caressed her cheek. "No matter what happens tonight, you must stay safe. Do you hear me? Listen to Joanna and Miss Atwell and stay alive."

Sarah had no intention of disobeying her bodyguards, but she appreciated how difficult it must be for Hart not to be her primary protector this night and to acknowledge it in front of others. "I will. And you must promise me the same."

"I promise." He said it with no hesitation, no impudent grin, just his eyes meeting hers.

The moment was broken when Joanna spoke. "Let's get you into the ballroom, my lady."

Sarah nodded, kissing her husband once more, placing her hand over his heart to feel the steel plates she'd helped him sew into his waistcoat, before releasing him and following Miss Atwell. Moving Sarah inside the ballroom gave her guards more room in the event of a fight, and it put her closer to her escape route through the French windows in case she had to run.

They made it to the center of the dance floor before the French windows crashed open, one of the glass panes shattering when the window frame impacted the wall. Rebecca stalked inside the ballroom, dragging one of the shorter footmen by the hair with the tip of a knife pressed to this throat. Her hair was not the golden blonde it had been but a dull brown, her clothes older and more worn than the daughter of an earl would ever wear.

"Looking for me?"

Joanna and Miss Atwell took up defensive positions on either side of Sarah. She prayed Hartland had the sense to get away.

"Yes, we are. Why don't you let Benson go, and you and I can talk." Benson had been one of the footmen assigned to protect her when she'd first become engaged to Hartland. He'd watched over her when the threat against her had been intangible. She couldn't allow him to be killed now that the threat was right here in their own ballroom.

Rebecca laughed, jostling the leather satchel slung over one of her shoulders as she adjusted the knife in her hand. "Of course, *my lady*. I'll release the only leverage I have and let you take me into custody, shall I?"

Sarah clenched her fingers around her steel fan, hoping Rebecca wouldn't see her hands shaking. Had Hartland's associates been alerted to Rebecca's presence in the ballroom? "We both know you've brought more weapons than just that knife. Release Benson, unharmed. You'll still be able to kill me from where you stand, and that will be leverage enough."

Rebecca glanced at the footman she held, then removed the knife from his throat. "He stays here, where I can see that he isn't passing messages to whomever else you have recruited to help you."

Benson's eyes met Sarah's and he nodded his agreement to the terms. Sarah had hoped for exactly what Rebecca wanted to prevent, that the footman would find Lord Thorston or Mr. Devlin outside and explain the situation. But this, at least, would put Benson out of immediate danger.

"Fine."

Rebecca opened the hand that held Benson's hair and shoved him away. He stumbled, careening into the glass of the broken French window. Once he'd righted himself, Sarah caught his eye again and shook her head the tiniest bit, hoping he wouldn't disobey Rebecca and dash out into the night. If he did, she'd certainly lose what little control she'd exhibited so far.

"Good. Now we can talk like civilized people." That was a phrase Sarah's mother had used whenever her father lost his temper and then regained it. Speaking with a mad bomber in the middle of a ballroom was hardly Mrs. Shipton's idea of civilized, but it was a step in the right direction for Sarah.

"Where is your husband?"

"What?" It was Sarah that Rebecca wanted dead, why was she asking for Hartland?

"Where is your husband?" Rebecca repeated, enunciating as if she were speaking to a slow-witted child. "I want him here, now."

"I'm here," a familiar voice called from the ballroom entrance.

Sarah's heart pounded, and the smooth fan slipped between her sweaty palms. The plan had been for Hartland to stay out of sight with Mr. Fortescue until they were needed. What on earth was he doing putting himself in danger?

"Nice distraction with the empty hackney, by the way," Hartland continued. Sarah didn't turn to watch him enter the room but kept her eyes on Rebecca, tracking his voice until he came to a halt beside Miss Atwell. "You knew no one would come to an event like this in a hired carriage, and that we'd be suspicious of it. Too bad you didn't pay the driver more—he told us about you without any resistance at all."

Rebecca's mouth turned down into a hard frown. "I might have known. I suppose you have your people waiting outside to take me into custody."

"I do.

"Then I'll have to be quick." She reached into her satchel and drew out a small pistol, aiming it at Hartland, and glass jar. "Do you know what this jar contains?"

It appeared empty, but it didn't take a genius to figure out what was really there. "It's phosgene, isn't it?"

"Enough to kill someone. All I have to do is smash it at your feet."

"You don't really want to do that, Rebecca," Hartland tried.

But that only seemed to make her angrier. "I know that I'm the wicked witch in this fairy story, that there will be no happy ending for me. All I want is to avenge David's death."

Her gaze swung to Sarah and she raised the glass jar as if to throw it. "I saw you kill him," she said, her voice breaking. "I watched you push him! Do you know what was in the box he carried?"

Sarah nodded slowly, fighting the lump that was growing in her throat.

"He lingered for three days. Three days of agony as his lungs filled with fluid and drowned him in his own bed."

A trio of gentlemen appeared outside the French windows dressed in eveningwear and laughing. Joanna tried to discreetly wave them away, but they either didn't see or didn't understand her signal and continued their approach.

There were tears coursing down Rebecca's face now, and Sarah felt her eyes prickling with her own tears. "You have to know it was an accident..."

"Well, this won't be."

The gentlemen were entering the ballroom as Rebecca took aim with her pistol once more. Sarah heard the *bang* of the gunshot and the *crash* of breaking glass. Miss Atwell pushed Hartland to the floor before Sarah could even scream his name, and Joanna grabbed her charge around the waist, propelling Sarah toward the French windows.

A muffled *pop* halted their movement for a moment, and the scent of new-mown hay began to drift through the air. Sarah's head jerked around—that was an odor that had no business being in a ballroom. Rebecca was lying on the floor with Benson atop her, her gun skittering across the marble.

Her leather satchel peeked out from beneath her torso.

"Everyone out!" Sarah yelled. "Phosgene is loose!"

She allowed Joanna to hustle her the rest of the way across the ballroom and out the French windows, waiting helplessly from the other side of the glass while others rushed in. Lord Thorston and Mr. Devlin grabbed Rebecca and Benson, Miss Atwell seized Hartland, and Joanna was scrambling to get the three guests out of the contaminated room.

Sarah imagined she could see the spread of the invisible phosgene throughout the ballroom. She "watched" it surround Rebecca and Benson, clinging to them as they were helped outside. It swirled around Hartland, too, invading his body through his nose and mouth as he gasped for air.

When Miss Atwell and Joanna finally brought him outside, Sarah directed them to set him down against the wall of the house and immediately began checking him for wounds. "Where are you hit?"

He raised his arm with a grimace, revealing a tear in his coat and waistcoat and a dent in the steel plate beneath. "Just a glancing blow. Benson hit her right before she pulled the trigger and fouled up her aim."

Sarah ran her unsteady fingers over the misshapen plate. "Oh, thank God."

"I think he's cracked another rib, though," Miss Atwell said, trying to catch her own breath.

"He likely should still be in bed from the last time," Joanna said, winking at Sarah. "Some people just don't know when rest is good for them."

"This time he will get all the rest he needs," Sarah vowed. "I will see to it myself."

Hart insisted on staying near the ballroom, giving orders for Rebecca to be detained under guard in one of Elliott House's guest bedrooms while they awaited the arrival of both a physician and the magistrate. When she wasn't coughing hard enough to injure herself, her breathing was rapid and shallow, her face contorted in pain. If she survived the night it would be a miracle.

The physician would see to Rebecca, but not before Benson was examined. The footman who'd brought her down was also in distress, his skin pale and clammy as he struggled to breathe. Hart didn't know if anything could be done for the young man, but that wouldn't stop him from trying. Not only had he saved his master's life, but Sarah's, Joanna's, and Elizabeth Atwell's, too, not to mention anyone else who might have entered the ballroom. He was the hero Hart couldn't be.

"Your turn," Sarah said to him, kneeling before him.

He tried to wave her away. "I'll be fine. Are you well?"

"I will be when the physician takes a look at you."

He would probably submit to that, eventually. "You first."

She nodded. "I will agree to that if you will at least let me help you get that waistcoat off."

He wasn't going to object. The dented steel plate was digging in to his newly cracked rib, and the pain it caused was making it rather difficult for him to act lordly. He allowed her to help him to his feet and peel his tailcoat from his shoulders, but insisted on unbuttoning his waistcoat himself. The last thing he needed after all this excitement was for his wife to undress him in the middle of their lawn.

"Here, let me..." She moved behind him and slid the waistcoat off his shoulders when his injuries limited his range of motion. "Do you want to put your tailcoat back on?"

"It would be more proper, wouldn't it?"

"Especially with all these people around." The ball continued in the redecorated outbuilding two hundred yards away, with guests emerging for the fireworks display, and most of the team they'd recruited had gathered behind the house. It would be beyond scandalous for anyone but Sarah to see him with just one layer—the layer nearest his skin—covering his chest.

"But it's a warm night," he grinned. "I think I'll leave it off."

"Then perhaps I can cover you up." She circled back around him and slipped her arms around his waist, dropping her forehead to his shoulder.

Another thing he wouldn't object to, even with the crowd. He wrapped his arms around her and kissed her temple. "Are you truly well?" he whispered.

"More or less," she replied quietly, even as her body trembled. "I've got some cuts from the glass jar Rebecca threw at me, but those will heal. I'm not so sure my mind has grasped all that has happened yet."

"Nor has mine," he confessed. There were still details to take care of, like putting the word out that there would no longer be a reward for Sarah's death, but for all practical purposes her ordeal was over. She was free.

She tightened her arms around him and he groaned involuntarily at the pressure on his injured ribs.

"Oh, I'm sorry."

She loosened her grasp immediately and started to back away, but he stroked a hand over her hair and drew her close to him again. "It's all right. Just hold me for a few more minutes, will you?"

She obliged and pressed herself against him, soft and pliant despite the trembling. He reciprocated, sheltering her in his arms. In an odd way, he drew strength from her distress. At that moment, he wanted nothing more than to be the strong, brave man she needed.

When Fortescue arrived with the protective clothing, Hart set his wife gently away from him. "I've got one more thing to do tonight, my love."

"Surely you aren't going in there again."

"I am."

She placed her hands on his shoulders and gave them a little squeeze. "Hartland, you can barely stand. Your breathing is labored. The very last place you should be is in a room full of poison."

"I have a promise to keep," he replied matter-of-factly.

But she was unconvinced. "You kept your promise—Rebecca is no longer a threat to me. I am safe."

"You are not safe near a room full of poison." He stroked her cheek, hoping he could convey his need to do this last thing for her with his eyes. "Let me fulfill my part of your plan."

She held his gaze for several long moments before she spoke again. "You allowed me to make my own choices this past month, even when it meant putting myself in danger. I suppose I should allow you the same freedom."

"Thank you."

"But don't forget the other promise you made me today." She slid her arms around his neck and whispered, "You must stay safe and come back to me alive."

He kissed her hair, her cheek, and whispered back, "I will. I swear it."

She insisted on helping him don his protective gear, like a squire of old preparing a knight for battle. Hart and Fortescue each wore a heavy leather apron and gauntlets procured from the forge beside Hartland's workshop, a pair of Hartland's sturdiest riding boots, and a damp rag tied over the nose and mouth. No one knew if it would be enough protection from the phosgene, but it was the best they could do—Hart still hadn't managed to make his own air-filtering mask work.

"Move slowly so you don't stir up the phosgene too much," Sarah instructed them. "It's heavier than air, so it will be more concentrated closer to the floor. When it breaks down, the carbonic oxide gas may rise up, and the muriatic acid should fall to the floor. If you hear fizzing, that's the acid reacting with the chalk, and you know the process is working."

She checked over the knots on the aprons and masks once more. "And neither of you is to stay inside that room for more than a few minutes at a time. When you come out, you will hand off your protective clothing to another man and get yourself away from the French windows. There's no way to tell how much phosgene is still in there."

Hart and Fortescue both nodded, and for once Hart had every intention of obeying orders. He needed to follow through on his part of the plan and ensure Sarah's safety, but he had no desire to kill himself in the process.

Each man stepped into the ballroom carrying a large glass jug of water—heavier than Hart remembered from their trial run, and pulling on his damaged ribs—fitted with a specially made spout that projected the liquid out at a distance. It was more forceful than Hart had wanted, but it was an older invention being pressed into use. And it served as a makeshift timepiece as well—when the jug was out of water, it was time for fresh air.

They opened the spouts and began spraying the room, and Hart held his breath. He'd had the ballroom floor chalked as was fashionable, hiring an artist to draw various flowers and animals across the floor, ostensibly for better footing during periods of dancing. A large portion of the chalk was being washed away by the too-forceful streams of water, but as Hart walked slowly around the room with Fortescue, he heard the quiet yet unmistakable sound of fizzing.

"It's working!" he called through his mask.

It was only a few minutes before both jugs were empty, and the damp cloths over their faces began to dry out. Hart and Fortescue made their way out of the ballroom and onto the lush grass, waiting until they were yards away from the French windows before they began to strip off their protection. Hart had forgotten just how hot one became wearing all that thick leather, and was thankful for the opportunity to get out of it.

Fortescue's betrothed, Miss Hale, came out to help him with the knots, and Sarah was three steps behind her.

"How do you feel?" Sarah asked, touching Hart's forehead, his cheek, any exposed skin she could find.

"I'm no worse than I was before," he answered, pulling the cloth from his face with a grin.

She stepped behind him and untied his mask and apron as he shed the bulky gauntlets. "Given the circumstances, that will do." Once the leather had been handed off to the next wearer, Sarah was in his arms again. "Thank you for keeping your promises," she murmured.

He seemed to ache from head to toe, but for just a few moments he ignored the pain and reveled in the moment. They were battered but not broken, victorious over their enemy. And Hart had the rest of his life to love Sarah.

Chapter Seventeen

Sarah stayed at Hartland's side as he convalesced at Elliott House, confined to bed for three weeks and given explicit instructions not to engage in what the physician had called his "marital duty." They played cards using the mattress as a table, they read aloud to each other from various texts, they even took their meals together in Hartland's bedchamber. And when his eyes began to droop, she climbed carefully onto the big bed and lay beside him as he slept, her own body healing alongside his.

He'd been granted a brief reprieve to attend Rebecca's funeral, but declined. The amount of phosgene she'd inhaled had rendered her lungs nearly useless before the physician had even arrived, and she'd died within a day of her attempted attack on Elliott House's ballroom. Mr. MacDonald took charge of her body, as she had no other relatives, and found a clergyman who would perform the service. He intended to bury her beside his brother, believing it would have been David's wish. But neither Hart nor Sarah desired to say a final goodbye to the woman who had tried to kill them both.

Once each week Hart was also allowed up to visit Benson, who was ensconced in a guest bedchamber in his own convalescence. Hartland swore he needed Sarah's help to walk the distance from his own chamber to Benson's, despite being fairly steady on his feet. Benson, on the other hand, was in a bad way. The physician was unsure if he would live, but if he did his lungs would be permanently damaged. He'd never work again, certainly; it was likely his life would never be normal, either.

"What else can I do for him?" Hart asked after the third visit.

Sarah shook her head. He'd already arranged for a generous pension for the young man if he survived and settled an annuity on his parents. "He cheers up considerably when you visit," she offered.

"He cheers up considerably when *you* visit," Hartland countered with a grin. "But I'll not be giving you over to him—or anyone else—anytime soon."

By the fourth week of his recovery the physician told Hartland he might begin spending time out of bed, as long as he was careful not to overtax himself. And Hartland disappeared into his workshop, politely but firmly refusing Sarah entrance.

She tried not to think the worst, but visions of her husband in a sleep-deprived frenzy plagued her despite her best effort, and a nagging little voice tried to convince her that Hartland had tired of her. When he asked her to stop sleeping beside him at night, she reflexively began making plans to live a life separate from his.

Mrs. Shipton remained in the north with Lord Thorston's family, and would continue on with them until word had spread that there would be no reward for Sarah's death, but when it was safe again Sarah would probably take her mother and go to one of the estates Hartland had set aside for her use. She was a countess with generous sums of pin money and social standing. If she wanted to purchase a home in Town, she could. If she wanted to re-open the bookshop, she could. If she wanted to set up her own laboratory and perform experiments to her heart's content, she could do that, too.

But her heart wouldn't *be* content without her Hart.

She tortured herself for nearly a week before summoning her courage and marching out to Hartland's workshop. If he was planning to send her to the country and resume his former life, then she deserved to know that. If she was being ridiculous and panicking for no reason, than she deserved to know that, too.

The door was open when she arrived, a warm breeze leftover from summer ruffling the flowers that had been planted along the outer wall. Hart stood with his hands on his hips, wearing a shirt, trousers, and stout boots, his sleeves rolled up above his elbows.

"What else does it need?"

"A woman's touch?" she said lightly, taking a few steps inside.

His head swung around. "Sarah! What are you doing out here?"

His voice was bright, if such a thing could be said of sound, almost as if he were trying to sound happy to see her when he was not.

"I came to see you. May I steal you away from your work for a few moments?"

He glanced back at the table where he'd been working and frowned, but managed a smile when he met Sarah's eyes. "May I show you something first?"

"Certainly." That he wanted to share his work with her was a good sign, wasn't it?

They met in the middle of the workshop and he reached for her hand. "I'd hoped to have this more complete before you saw it, but since you're already here..."

She allowed him to take her hand and lead her to the other side of the room. He'd pushed several battered old tables together to form a large workbench, complete with notebooks and pencils, a few leather-bound books, and assorted glassware similar to what she'd used when testing the muriatic acid.

"What do you think?"

"It's much neater than your usual workspace," she said with a chuckle.

"Will it do?"

Sarah shifted her eyes from the tables to her husband. "For what?"

"For you, my lady." His mouth was curved into a half-smile, but his brows had risen toward his hairline. "Do you like it?"

"Oh, Hart..." She twined her arm with his and took a better look at the space he'd created for her.

Nearly a third of the workshop had been cleared of everything except the tables, a couple of stools, and implements he'd gathered for her use. "You're giving me part of your workshop?"

"We can have something built if you'd like privacy or solitude," he responded, his smile growing. "And I'll have something similar done for you at Hartland Abbey and Glanmire House. But I thought this would be a good start if you wanted to put that chemistry knowledge in your head to practical use, or have a sunny place to work on your embroidery. Or maybe to work on a few things with me. Whatever you might want the space for."

She wrapped her arms around him, careful not to squeeze his healing torso too tightly, and pressed a kiss to his cheek. "I love it."

He held her against him for much too short a time, then loosened his arms and drew away from her. "I'm afraid I've also done something rather scandalous."

Ah, so that's what this was really about. He was trying to soften her up before admitting his blunder. "What is it this time?"

"I've fallen in love with my wife." He ran a hand over cheek and down her neck, caressing her skin with the pads of his fingers. "I'll give you an aristocratic marriage if you still want it, but I love you, Sarah Elliott. Will you stay with me and be my wife in truth, not just in name?"

"Yes!" She flew into his arms, trailing kisses across his temple and jaw until she reached his mouth. "I love you, too, my Hart," she murmured before capturing his lips with hers.

It had been more than a month since they'd last been intimate, and Sarah could feel his arousal pressing against her. She broke away, borrowing one of Hart's signature grins. "Does this mean we'll be sharing a bed again?"

"Is that hope in your voice, my love?"

"It most certainly is. Why did you send me away in the first place?"

His hand slid down her back and cupped her bottom, pressing her more firmly against him. "Because the physician forbade vigorous activity of any sort. When I was too sore to move much, it was easier to resist the temptation. But since I've been feeling better, I wasn't sure if we would be able to comply with his orders."

The relief must have shown on her face because he continued, "You didn't think I'd taken a mistress, did you?"

"I didn't know what to think. You have to give me some context when you do perplexing things like that."

"I don't have a mistress. I haven't since before we were wed, and I never will again. I don't want anyone but you in my bed." He punctuated the statement with a kiss that chased away any remaining doubt in her mind.

"Good," she gasped, drawing back to catch her breath while he feathered kisses down her neck. "Because the only lover I want is you, no matter how many children we have."

"Then we are agreed," he mumbled, opening the top buttons on her gown and pressing his warm lips to her bare shoulder.

"We are," she sighed. "Shall we defy your physician's orders after all?"

He straightened with a laugh, the corners of his eyes crinkling up as he gazed down at her. "Lady Hartland, rule breaker. Who am I to say no to that?"

Just a few days later, Hartland walked out to the workshop he now shared with his wife in an effort to locate her. He found her standing at her workbench, a pile of cloth scraps to her left, a box of matches in her hand, and a metal bowl in front of her.

"Sarah, my love, what are you doing?"

She kept her eyes on the tableau before her, striking a match and dropping it into the bowl. "Trying to find a good way to make your brigandines less prone to catch fire. I've mixed up a few recipes to treat the fabric, but I need to find out which one works the best."

He waved a hand in front of his face as he crossed the room. "Whatever that one was, cross it off the list. It stinks."

She reached for a pitcher and poured water on the offending material. "Noted. Did you need me for something?"

"Lady Stirling's ball?" It wasn't a large gathering, but Hart and Sarah had agreed to attend. It would be their first time in public since Rebecca's final attack, and neither was sure how they'd feel being in a ballroom again.

Her face lit with recognition. "Is it time to go already?"

He nodded, taking the matches from her and setting them down on the battered old table. "You have twenty minutes to ready yourself, though your maid seems to think you'll need more time than that."

"Lucy always worries that my hair will take too long to dress," Sarah smiled. "Just let me put these materials away, and I'll go right in."

Hart helped with the cleanup and escorted his wife from the workshop back to the house, then on to the carriage when she had completed her toilette. She'd chosen a silk ball gown that matched the bottle green waistcoat he wore, right down to the velvet embellishments. Was that a coincidence, or was his wife colluding with his valet?

He brushed the thought away when he took his seat beside her in the carriage, clasping her gloved hand in his.

"Ready?"

"Yes, I suppose so." Her voice was steady when she spoke, but her eyes were focused on his cravat rather than his face.

"We don't have to go," he reminded her. It wasn't as if the fate of the realm hung in the balance this evening.

She smiled dutifully and met his gaze. "It will be good for both of us to be among people again and just be someone's guests."

"But if you aren't ready..."

The focus these past weeks had mainly been on Hart's recovery from the gunshot and Sarah's from the attempted strangulation. No one had thought much about the mental harm the death threats and assaults had done to either of them, and he certainly didn't want to put Sarah in a position she wasn't yet comfortable with.

She squeezed his hand and scooted closer to him. "I am. And if it all gets to be too much, we'll simply leave early."

"You know I'd never refuse the chance to leave a ball early," he grinned. Though perhaps this one, with Sarah on his arm, would be different.

It wasn't, at least not in the beginning. The line of carriages waiting to get to Lady Stirling's door was as tiresome as the receiving line. But once they entered the actual ballroom, the evening began to look up.

"Look, there's Diana," Sarah said, waving to her friend.

Hart still didn't know Diana Talbot terribly well, but he felt the change in his wife's demeanor as they walked across the ballroom. Her posture relaxed, her grip on his arm loosened, and her lips curved into a genuine smile.

"If it isn't Lord and Lady Hartland," Miss Talbot said, grinning as they approached. When they'd exchanged the requisite greetings, she lowered her voice. "I've only just come back to Town myself. After that threatening letter arrived, Lord Preston sent me to his sister in Shrewsbury—he thought I'd be out of danger there. I'll admit I had a lovely time, but it meant we had to change my wedding date. You've received the new invitation?"

Thankfully, Sarah handled that question and Hart wasn't required to chime in at all. A wave of regret passed over him as Miss Talbot went on to describe the preparations for her wedding with the enthusiasm of a child opening long-expected gifts. Had Sarah looked forward to arranging her own wedding day with such eagerness?

"One more thing, Diana," Sarah was saying when Hart forced his attention back to the conversation. "Why did you think to introduce me to Hartland in the first place?"

"What is this, now?" he asked, arching an eyebrow.

Miss Talbot giggled. "Sarah found out about her mother's finances just before my betrothal ball, and I offered to introduce her to eligible gentlemen with means. You merely met the criteria, my lord. I never expected anything would come of it, but your marriage seems to have been good for you both."

"That it has," Sarah replied, glancing at Hart.

He nodded, unable to keep from grinning at his wife. "I would agree."

"I would also agree," another voice chimed in. It was the Marquess of Preston, appearing very self-satisfied. "I didn't think you had it in you, Hartland, but your lady wife looks happy."

"I am, my lord," Sarah offered with a grin.

Hart tried not to scowl. Yes, he would love Sarah until the day he died, but there was no need to be smug about it. "I did tell you that we'd rub along well enough together. It turns out, I was right."

Preston laughed and took Miss Talbot off to search for her mother, while Hartland wandered into the card room, leaving Sarah on her own in the ballroom. He'd have preferred to stay by her side, but convention dictated that they socialize separately for most of the evening, and she'd wanted to have as normal an outing as possible.

"I will be fine," she told him, flattening a wayward lapel on his tailcoat. "And if I become distressed, I'll find you."

"Very well then."

"Make me the same promise?"

He'd been in enough life-or-death situations that he liked to think nothing bothered him anymore, but that wasn't strictly true. "I promise to come find you if I need to."

They ended up meeting only twice that night, once for a sedate quadrille and once for an energetic country dance. But when the supper dance came along and the clock approached midnight, Sarah rescued him from a group of gentlemen bent on talking politics. Hart excused himself and offered her his arm.

"Do you know that it's possible to be bored to death?" he asked when they were seated in the carriage. "I could feel the life actually draining from my body."

Sarah laughed and cuddled up to him, resting her head on his shoulder. "I'll take boring over the likes of Rebecca any day."

"Absolutely." He kissed the top of her head and wrapped his arm around her. "But something more stimulating than the election would be nice."

"Something like one of your special messengers?"

"They do bring news more stimulating than the election." He'd had an idea about those messengers when he'd gone to fetch Sarah from their workshop, but hadn't had a chance to broach the subject in her rush to get ready. "May I ask you a question?"

"You just did."

He didn't need to see her face to know that she was smirking at him, and he grinned back. "I love you, do you know that?"

"Yes," she answered contentedly. "What did you want to ask me?"

"How would you feel about helping me from time to time with the letters the special messengers bring?" He didn't tell her about Wellington's intelligence gathering ring, nor would he involve her in ferreting out the tidbits he passed along. But her strengths compensated for his weaknesses, making him safer when he was out as the Armored Man.

"What would I do?"

He counted the possibilities off on his fingers, even though she couldn't see them in the dark. "Help me plan my strategy when a problem arises. Explain things to me when chemistry is involved.

Remind me not to be an idiot when I confront a lawbreaker."

She sat up, bracing herself against his chest. "Go with you to confront the lawbreakers?"

"Possibly." He winced. It wasn't that he didn't trust her to keep her wits about her in times of danger, he just didn't want to put her in danger in the first place. "If you were properly equipped and trained. You need more than a steel-plated corset and a few defensive moves first."

Without warning, her lips found his and her arms came around his neck. "Thank you," she murmured. "I don't know if I want to put myself in harm's way, even to save lives, but thank you for letting me make the choice. I love you for that...and for so many other reasons."

He wrapped his arms around her and pulled her onto his lap, closing his eyes and inhaling the scent of lemon verbena that clung to her skin. "I may not be the man you would have chosen, but I will never stop trying to make you happy."

"You don't have to try, my love. You already have."

How did he get so lucky? He was so much better with her than he was without her, and all she asked in return was that he continue to be the best version of himself.

"Is this what marriage is supposed to be, then?" he chuckled, nuzzling her neck. "Two people head over ears in love with each other, keeping each other safe?"

She ran her fingers through his hair and laid her cheek against his. "It's what our marriage will be."

About the Author

Cora Lee is National Bestselling author of Regency romance. She went on a twelve year expedition through the blackboard jungle as a high school math teacher before publishing Save the Last Dance for Me, the first book in the Maitland Maidens series. She then followed it up with eight more novels and novellas, ranging from sweet and traditional to spicy and suspenseful.

When she's not walking Rotten Row at the fashionable hour or attending the entertainments of the Season, you might find her participating in Regency Fiction Writers events, wading through her towering TBR pile, or eagerly awaiting the next Marvel movie release.

Other Books By Cora Lee

Sweet & Traditional:

Save the Last Dance for Me (Maitland Maidens #1)
Back In My Arms Again (Maitland Maidens #2)
Kissing by the Mistletoe (Maitland Maidens #3)
A Kiss to Build a Dream On (Maitland Maidens #4)
When I Fall In Love (Maitland Maidens #5)

Spicy and Suspenseful:

No Rest for the Wicked
The Good, The Bad, And The Scandalous
The Duke of Darkness